D0350442

The world is in peril.

An ancient evil is rising from beneath
Erdas, and we need YOU to help stop it.

Claim your spirit animal and join the
adventure now:

1. Go to scholastic.com/spiritanimals.

2. Log in to create your character and
   choose your own spirit animal.

3. Have your book ready and enter the
   code below to unlock the adventure.

Your code: ND62D7JN3W

By the Four Fallen,
The Greencloaks

"Tell Dawson
I was a hero."

THE WILDCAT'S CLAW

FALL of the BEASTS
SPIRIT ANIMALS

THE WILDCAT'S CLAW

Varian Johnson

SCHOLASTIC INC.

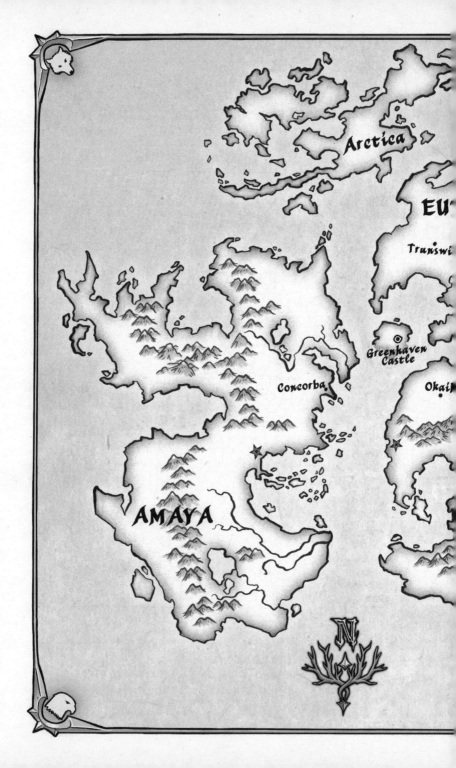

Arctica

EU

Trunswi

Greenhaven
Castle

Concorba

Okai

AMAYA

ERDAS

The
Petral
Mountains

ZHONG

Jano
Rion

NILO

OCEANUS

Hundred
Isles

The Evertree

Stetriol

For Crystal, who gives us treats
even when we misbehave–VJ

Library of Congress Control Number: 2017941615

ISBN 978-1-338-18982-7

10 9 8 7 6 5 4 3 2 1   17 18 19 20 21

Book design by Charice Silverman
Library edition, October 2017

Printed in the U.S.A. 23

Scholastic US: 557 Broadway • New York, NY 10012
Scholastic Canada: 604 King Street West • Toronto, ON M5V 1E1
Scholastic New Zealand Limited: Private Bag 94407 • Greenmount, Manukau 2141
Scholastic UK Ltd.: Euston House • 24 Eversholt Street • London NW1 1DB

THE WILDCAT'S CLAW

LENORI

LENORI PACED HER CRAMPED QUARTERS—WHICH WERE little more than a small, single holding cell with meager wood furnishings. She hadn't had contact with Olvan, or any other Greencloaks, since being imprisoned. Most of the others had been captured and returned to Greenhaven Castle, where they would be held for trial, but she and Olvan remained in the Council Citadel.

Olvan.

He'd been struck by a stone viper's fangs, and most of his body was turned to stone. Thanks to her rainbow ibis, Myriam, Lenori could sense his presence. He was in pain, but alive, though she didn't know for how long.

She didn't know how long any of them had.

The Second Devourer War had taken a heavy toll on all the nations, and the Wyrm's destructive reign of terror only amplified people's fears. The Greencloaks had saved the world, but it had come at a great price. Despite their best efforts, many people had suffered.

Zerif, under the Wyrm's control, had used his immense powers to ravage the world. But these battles weren't just fought in far-off lands like Stetriol or Arctica. There was bloodshed in every village. Neighbor against neighbor. Brother against brother. Mother against daughter. Father against son.

The Greencloaks themselves had inflicted some of the worst damage.

Zerif, armed with the Wyrm's parasites, had taken control of most of their order, and had then turned them loose to wreak havoc in every corner of every land. There was no village, no militia, and no army that could prevail against a legion of Greencloaks when they partnered with their spirit animals. With their true, uninhibited powers now unleashed, the Greencloaks had shown the world just how powerful they'd become.

People were afraid of them. They were angry. They were distrustful. And Lenori couldn't fault any of them for feeling that way.

She and Olvan thought that by coming here to meet with the leaders of the nations, they would be able to soothe any doubts and remind the world that the Greencloaks only wanted to preserve peace. They had even brought along the Four Heroes of Erdas—each from a different nation, but united in their oath to serve and protect all lands. But thanks to traitors within their midst, the Emperor of Zhong had fallen, and the real Greencloaks were left to take the blame.

Lenori pressed her ear against the door to make sure that no one was nearby, but heard only a quiet dripping from the Citadel's leaking roof. She released Myriam from passive state. The ibis strutted around, proudly displaying her rainbow feathers and shaking her long, thin legs.

"No time for showing off, Myriam," Lenori said. "We must find our young friends."

She sat down on the stone floor and closed her eyes. She pushed the cold of the room, the fear of her imprisonment, and the worry for her fellow Greencloaks from her mind. Her pulse slowed and her body relaxed. It was just her, Myriam, and Erdas, united as one.

A hazy image floated before her. She concentrated, trying to sharpen its edges. Trying to bring it into focus. It was a ship, cutting across the ocean. Squeezing her eyes tighter, she saw the Four Heroes huddled in a small room. No—not four. There were six of them. They had been tested recently—she could see the weariness of their faces—but they exuded a sense of accomplishment. Her mind centered itself on Rollan. Her gaze fell to the thin leather strap around his neck.

The Heart of the Land. He had revealed it!

She heard something in the distance. Echoes? Footsteps?

Was there danger on the boat? A trap waiting to be sprung?

She shook her head. Those sounds weren't coming from the ship. Someone was approaching her room.

She blinked, and her mind returned to her cell. She looked at the ibis, sitting calmly beside her. "Myriam, back to me. I don't want them to know that you've been loose."

The rainbow ibis disappeared just as the heavy wooden door swung open. Two Oathbound warriors, both dressed in black, entered the room. She recognized the one with the short blond hair. Sure enough, the woman's brown stone viper flashed into view, curling around her large arm. Brunhild the Merry. She was the one who'd poisoned Olvan.

The other warrior was new to Lenori. Like Brunhild, this woman wore a black uniform with brass neck and wrist collars, but the woman also sported shiny, gaudy rings on most of her fingers. Her long brown hair was twisted into an intricate braid that trailed over her shoulder, like an embroidered rope hanging from a curtain.

The unknown woman snapped her fingers, and a servant entered the room, carrying a tray full of breads, dates, and cheeses. Lenori willed her stomach to remain silent. It was the first food she'd seen in two days.

The servant placed the tray before Lenori, then left the room. The woman with the long braid took a step forward. "Don't you want to eat?"

Lenori pretended that the food wasn't there. "No, I want to be set free."

The braided woman shook her head. "Don't ask for the impossible," she said. "Go on, take a bite. Eat it all. Gorge yourself." She grinned. "I promise it isn't laced with stone viper venom."

Lenori instead curled her hands into her lap. "What do you want from me?"

"We know why your young friends were in Amaya," the Oathbound woman said, whipping her braid over her shoulder and behind her back. She began to pace, her boots echoing on the scarred stone bricks. "For such a small amulet, it carries quite a punch. The children were lucky to escape with it." She pulled a red-tinged sword from her side. It sparkled as light hit its blade. "We've heard reports that they're on a ship headed for Eura," she said. "What's there? Another of these so-called gifts?"

Lenori stared ahead, saying nothing.

The woman knelt so that she and Lenori were face-to-face. Her hazel eyes were as cold as the floor. Then she placed her sword on the ground, well within Lenori's reach. It was almost as if the woman were daring Lenori to try to grab it.

"I understand that you don't want to betray your friends," the woman said. "But they're just children. They shouldn't be fighting these battles. Take pity on them. Spare them any further pain and hardship."

"They've saved the world twice," Lenori said. "You should not underestimate them."

The woman inspected her own hands, tracing her fingertips across her numerous rings. The ring on her middle finger was adorned with three small, cone-shaped spikes. She twisted the ring so the spikes pointed from the inside of her hand. Then, with a wry smile creeping across her face, the woman slapped Lenori. Lenori cried out, more from the shock than the pain. Then the woman struck Lenori again, even harder. Lenori's face burned. The woman's ring had left its mark.

"And you should not underestimate me," the woman replied as she twisted her blood-tipped ring back into place.

Lenori let her gaze flicker to the sword lying on the floor. She considered lunging for it, but stopped herself. She was sure that was exactly what the woman wanted. Lenori refused to give her the satisfaction.

Leaving the sword on the floor, the woman picked up a loaf of bread. She tore off a small piece, then popped it into her mouth. "Delicious." Then she held the bread under Lenori's nose. "I know you want a bite. You must be delirious with hunger."

Lenori shook her head.

The woman sighed, then ate a larger piece. "Where are they going, Lenori? What are they searching for? Is there another gift out there? Is it just as powerful as the Heart of the Land?" The woman dropped the remaining bread on the tray, picked up her sword, and returned to her feet. "I promise, if you help me, I will capture them safely and return them unharmed." The woman glanced at Brunhild. "You know what happened to Olvan. I would hate for a similar fate to befall those children."

"You'll never find them," Lenori said.

For the first time since entering the room, the woman stopped smiling. "Perhaps another two days without food will help you change your mind." She snapped her fingers, and the Oathbound warrior returned. Lenori's insides seized as he picked up the tray.

The braided woman held up her hand, signaling the warrior to stop. With her sword, she sliced off a minuscule hunk of cheese. Barely enough to fill a thimble.

"On second thought, why don't you keep a piece," she said, tossing the food at Lenori. It bounced off her leg and landed on the floor beside her. Specks of dirt covered the once pristine cheese.

"See how kind I am? I could have left you with nothing." The woman stepped out of the room. "But like that food, my kindness will not last forever. Tell me what I want to know, or prepare yourself for death."

The door slammed shut, leaving Lenori in silence. She picked up the small slice of cheese. Her mouth watered. . . . It smelled even better once in her hands.

Then, slowly, she ground the food between her fingers, disintegrating it.

Her faith may be tested, but she would not falter.

She was a Greencloak.

Committed to the end, no matter what.

2

ACROSS THE OCEAN

CONOR GLANCED OUT OF THE PORTHOLE OF THE SLEEK clipper as it sliced through choppy seas and strong winds. They had boarded the boat in a small coastal town just north of Concorba. Thanks to a small collection of coins from Worthy—and Rollan's skill with negotiations—they had been able to secure a cabin with four beds, along with two packs of meager provisions. The room wasn't nearly big enough for all six of them to comfortably sleep at one time, but Conor and his friends weren't in the position to be choosy.

Stepping closer to the window, Conor squinted at his reflection in the dirty, smudged glass. He reached to his forehead and ran his fingers along his skin, right where the mark of the Wyrm used to be. The black, swirling mark had faded from view, but he could still feel its power. Its weight. It was an invisible burden he feared he would carry for the rest of his life.

"See anything of interest?" a voice asked behind him.

Smiling, he turned around. Abeke was always light on her feet, even with Uraza, her leopard, in passive state on her arm. Conor flexed his own forearm, watching his muscles ripple underneath Briggan's mark. He hated leaving the Great Wolf in passive state for so long, but their current mission required stealth, not strength.

Conor looked back out the window and stared into the distance. "It could be a mirage, but I think I see land in the distance."

"I just spoke with the captain," she said. "We'll reach port soon."

Conor grinned. Eura. Green fields. Light-blue skies and a cool breeze on his face. "Do you think I'll be able to see my family?" Conor asked. Although he had seen them recently, he always loved spending time with his parents and brothers. He didn't even mind getting up early in the morning to herd and shear the sheep. Seeing his family helped remind Conor that as a Greencloak, he not only fought to protect Erdas, he also fought to protect those closest to him.

"I could show you guys a real Euran meal," he continued. "Shepherd's pie and all."

Abeke frowned, which was more than enough of an answer for him. Rollan had gone to see his mother in Amaya, and as a result, the Oathbound had almost captured them. If it wasn't for Worthy, they probably wouldn't have escaped.

Abeke saw something in his face—perhaps worry for his family—because she suddenly smiled and said, "Maybe the bounties put out for us by the Oathbound haven't yet reached all parts of Erdas. If so, and if time allows, I'm sure you'll be able to see your family. And it would be nice to have a normal meal for once." She turned to their friends, still asleep. "We should wake the others."

"You wake up Rollan," Conor said, pointing to one of the cots on the other side of the room. "He's always cranky when he doesn't get enough sleep."

Conor went to rouse Worthy and Anka while Abeke crossed their quarters. Worthy was curled into a fetal position on his bed, his red cloak draped over his body. Conor wasn't sure, but he thought that he might have been purring in his sleep.

"Get up, Worthy," Conor said, giving him a slight nudge.

The Redcloak yawned and stretched, his golden eyes blinking behind his white, cat-shaped mask. Worthy tried to stand, but became unbalanced with the shifting of the ship. He slowly sank back to the flat mattress. "You should have woken me when we reached land."

Conor shook his head. In addition to his heightened reflexes and strength, Worthy had also gained his former spirit animal's dislike of water—and a black tail that he preferred no one talk about. Conor wondered what other traits Worthy had inherited when he merged with the wildcat. Hopefully he wouldn't start shedding or hacking up hairballs.

Anka stirred in the bunk beside Worthy. At least Conor assumed it was Anka. Thanks to her chameleon's powers, she had blended in with the threadbare blue blanket covering her, making her almost invisible to the eye. As she sat up, her skin shifted from the muted blue to a warm brown, matching the planks on the cabin walls.

Across the room, Meilin and Rollan yawned. Meilin jumped out of bed, but Rollan remained in the adjacent bunk, pulling his thick brown cloak around him and squeezing his eyes shut. The cloak had seemed too warm for Amaya, but it would serve him well on their journey through Eura. Conor knew how cold the nights could get, and he wondered if they had been too hasty in leaving their trusty green cloaks along the roadside in Amaya.

"I don't always agree with Worthy, but he kind of has a point," Rollan said. "How about you wake us up when we get there?"

Meilin leaned over and thumped Rollan's ear. "Don't you want breakfast?"

Rollan groaned. "Salted flounder and stale biscuits. For the tenth day in a row." He faked a smile. "Yum."

Meilin thumped his ear again. "You've had worse. Remember that meal of seal fat in the Ardu settlement?"

"Don't remind me," he said, rubbing his ear. "I'll take the fish."

"First things first," Anka said, rising from the bed, her skin a transparent blur. "Worthy, now would be a good time for you to fill us in on everything you know about the next gift."

Worthy leaned back against the wall with his hands behind his head. He had seemed to enjoy withholding this information from them, probably because he wanted to make himself feel more important. For Worthy's sake, Conor hoped that he really knew where the next gift was. If not, Meilin was liable to toss him overboard.

Worthy's gaze settled on Conor. "Do you remember the stories about the great Euran warrior and his black wildcat?" he asked him.

Conor nodded. "A little. The rumors were that the wildcat was as large as Tellun."

"No, even larger," Worthy said. "The beast's booming roar was as loud as a thousand erupting volcanoes. Its fur was as dark as midnight during a lunar eclipse, and its diamond-forged claws and teeth could shred the densest of rock."

"I bet it couldn't slice the armor of the famous Amayan gila monster," Rollan mumbled.

Meilin, who was now sitting on the bed beside Rollan, jutted her elbow into his side. "Hush," she warned.

"There was also a rumor about the warrior wielding a powerful sword," Worthy continued. "Its hilt contained a yellow gem that matched the beast's eyes. And its blade was supposedly as sharp as the black wildcat's claws." Worthy paused. "That's what they called it: the Wildcat's Claw."

"Do you know where this sword is?" Abeke asked.

He shook his head. "We used to have a replica of the sword at Trunswick Manor. I used it during the war—that is, until it broke. So much for it being forged from the finest Trunswick iron. Anyway, while it wasn't the real thing, my father kept all sorts of journals and histories about our local legends at the manor. It was sort of an obsession of his. His library would be the best place to research the location of the real Wildcat's Claw."

Conor had remembered seeing the replica of this sword, but only once, when he was working as a servant to Worthy. Worthy had just been the spoiled Devin Trunswick back then, and Conor had been a simple shepherd's son. How times had changed.

"Without any other leads, it seems like our best course of action is to travel to Trunswick," Meilin said. She had risen from the bed, and was now spinning a quarterstaff around herself. "Hopefully we can find the records that will lead us to the real sword."

Conor knew he was beaming, and he didn't even try to hide it. *Trunswick!* Perhaps he would be able to see his family after all. They lived close to the city, easily within a day's travel.

"We'll need more supplies," Abeke said. "The weather will not be as forgiving as Amaya."

"There are plenty of trading posts on the way to Trunswick," Worthy said. "I think I have enough money to get us what we need."

"Yes, thank you for that," Anka said. "After so many days on the road, it was nice to sleep in a real bed."

"Don't thank me," he said. "Thank the Redcloaks. Shane left us a small fortune when he . . . you know . . ."

Conor was glad that Worthy didn't finish his statement. Abeke had turned toward the wall, away from them. Shane, the former leader of the Redcloaks, had died while fighting against the Wyrm. Abeke didn't speak of him much, but she'd cared greatly for him, even if those feelings were complicated.

"We'll need a lot more than clothing," Anka said. "We need food, weapons, supplies." She leaned against the door, blending in with the splintered wood. "Instead of traveling directly to Trunswick, we should first gather supplies at the Redcloak headquarters. You said they're close, correct?"

Worthy tugged at his collar. "I don't think that's a good idea," he said.

"I agree," Abeke said. "We need to find the next gift as quickly as we can. The longer we wait, the more dangerous it becomes for us and the rest of the Greencloaks."

Rollan cleared his throat. "Look, I'm not a big fan of the Redcloaks—no offense, Worthy—but maybe Anka has a point. It would be nice to get some decent food—something better than flounder, anyway. And maybe some more arrows for Abeke." He glanced at Meilin as she continued to spin her quarterstaff. "And maybe something with a blade for Meilin."

Rollan had been forced to throw in Meilin's sword as part of the deal when he booked the team's passage. She had swiped the sword off an Oathbound in Amaya, and had boasted about using the blade on Wikam the Just whenever they faced off again. Even though Meilin was perfectly capable of besting most warriors without *any* weapons, Conor and the others always breathed a little easier when Meilin was well-armed—especially when they were facing an army as large as the Oathbound.

Meilin stopped spinning her quarterstaff. "The Redcloaks *are* formidable warriors," she said, almost begrudgingly. "And there are a lot of Oathbound out there, and only six of us."

Worthy stood and moved to the center of the room. "They didn't hold off all those Oathbound in Amaya for us to just show up at their front door," he said. "We all know we're being tracked. The last thing I want to do is lead the Oathbound to the Redcloaks. If we fail, the Redcloaks will need to be ready to protect Erdas in our place."

"Whoa! Hold on there, buddy," Rollan said. "I just want the Redcloaks'* help *temporarily.* Erdas doesn't need their protection full time. That's why there are Greencloaks."

"You mean the Greencloaks currently locked up in Greenhaven Castle?" Worthy asked. "The Greencloaks jailed at the Citadel?"

"Enough," Abeke said. "We're supposed to be the glue, remember? We need to stick together, not fight." She turned to Conor. "You've been quiet. What do you think? Should Worthy take us to the Redcloak base?"

It took Conor a moment to realize that Abeke was talking to him. He was still caught up in the conversation, in hearing his friends argue with one another. If they weren't successful in saving the Greencloaks, it could soon be them *fighting* against one another, split among their home nations' armies. Conor against Abeke. Eura against Nilo. Nation against nation. There was no way that Erdas would survive that.

"How far away is the Redcloak headquarters?" he asked.

"At least a week's journey," Worthy said. "And that's if we can travel during the day. It would be much longer if we have to sneak around at night."

Conor rubbed his arm. He wished Briggan were at his side. He was always more at peace with the wolf beside him. Just running his hands through Briggan's luxurious gray-white fur calmed him. "We can't afford to lose that much time," he said. "I think we should head directly to Trunswick. But if we can't find anything, Worthy takes us to Redcloak headquarters to regroup and come up with a new plan."

Everyone slowly nodded in agreement. The glue holding them together was still there, at least for now.

"Enough talk," Rollan said, clapping his hands. "Who's up for some stale biscuits?"

After breakfast, which unfortunately was more fish scales than meat, Conor took to the deck of the ship, dodging deckhands as they prepared for landing. A fog had descended over the sea, surrounding the boat and slowing its progress. Conor could no longer see land, but he knew it was there.

He heard the boat's floorboards creak behind him. Turning, he saw Worthy slowly making his way toward him.

"For being part cat, you're not very quiet," Conor said. "You should take lessons from Abeke."

Worthy snorted at a few sailors as they sped by, their eyes on the ground the entire time. The crew had been leery of him ever since they'd left port—the eyes and the mask made him stand out more than the others. Worthy put on a good show, but Conor knew that the whispers and judging looks bothered him. He'd spent enough time with Worthy—and Devin—to recognize when things got under his skin.

Worthy leaned against the railing, then clutched it as the boat lurched again, his claws lodging themselves into the cracked wood. "We're close," he said. "I can smell land, even over all this salt water." He glanced at Conor. "Look, I just wanted to thank you for taking my side back in our cabin."

Technically, Conor hadn't taken anyone's side. He just wanted to get to Trunswick as quickly as possible.

"During our meal, Abeke mentioned that you'd spent time with your family before joining the Greencloaks at the Citadel," Worthy said. "Did you, um, make it into town?"

Conor shook his head. "No, I mostly stayed close to home. It didn't seem smart to travel into Trunswick." Even though the Wyrm had been defeated, people were still distrustful of men in uniform, especially Greencloaks. For many Eurans, the Greencloaks were just like the Conquerors, only more powerful.

"There's probably something you should know," Worthy began. "I . . . well . . . I kind of don't know where the records are that will lead us to the Wildcat's Claw."

"What?"

"You see, there was a fire at the manor. It was the only way to protect Dawson." Worthy shook his head. "It's hard to explain. I was having a really bad day."

Conor couldn't believe what he was hearing. "So where are we supposed to look?" he asked.

"My father probably saved his library before he was run out of town. I hope. The fire wasn't that bad. The last I saw, it had only consumed the top of the castle. And maybe the west wing. And the servants' quarters."

"The more you talk, the worse this sounds." Conor started to walk off. "I need to tell the others—"

"No! Wait." Worthy jumped in front of him. He blinked his catlike eyes at Conor. "Please don't tell them. I want them to trust me."

"You don't gain people's trust by lying to them."

"I know, it's just . . ." He shook his head. "I just want to be important. I want to be . . ."

"Worthy?"

He nodded. "I want to be a hero, like you all." He sighed. "The records are there somewhere. I'm sure."

Conor stared at Worthy for a long moment. He wished he could see the boy's face. His mask hid too much, making it hard for Conor to read him. Finally, Conor nodded. "Fine. We'll keep this between us for now." He looked back into the fog. "I just hope you're right about those records. All of Erdas is depending on it."

3

THE COUNTRYSIDE

THE FULL MOON ILLUMINATED THE OTHERWISE DARK sky as Meilin and the others departed the ship. Once they were a safe distance away from the pier, Abeke and Conor released their spirit animals. Briggan rolled in the tall grass, still damp from fog, then yelped like a pup playing with a bone. Conor scolded him at first, but then dropped down and tackled him, wrapping his arms around the wolf as if he were a toy instead of a Great Beast.

Uraza pawed the grass cautiously, then sniffed the air. Her ears perked up, her purple irises narrowed, and the fur rose on the scruff of her neck.

"I smell it, too," Abeke said, pulling an arrow from her quiver. "We'll be back in a second," she whispered to the others. "We're off to catch our next meal."

As they slipped away, Rollan looked toward the sky and watched as Essix looped through the air. Finally, she flew to his shoulder, settling on the heavy brown cloak. Unlike the other animals, Essix had chosen to remain free, only returning to the ship when she

19

needed a rest. Rollan pulled out a piece of dried fish and offered it to the bird. The gyrfalcon picked at the food, then squawked. Splaying her brownish-gold wings wide, she took to the air again, leaving the limp piece of meat in Rollan's fingers.

"See, even Essix is tired of fish," he mumbled. He took a bite of it, frowned, then spit it out.

"Are you going to release Jhi?" Anka asked Meilin. Anka was hidden, just a ripple beside her. She had taken on the characteristics of her surroundings, and was now just as dark as the nighttime sky.

"We should get moving," Meilin said. "I'll release her once we set up camp."

Anka placed her hand on Meilin's shoulder. "It's okay. I think we can spare a few minutes if you want to see her."

Meilin smiled. It *would* be good to see Jhi, even if only for a few moments. A flash struck the sky, and then there was Jhi, a mountain of black and white standing before her. Meilin placed her hands on the panda's plush fur. Jhi was warm—Meilin could have curled up against her right then. Jhi gave the girl a playful lick, making Meilin laugh.

"Yes, I've missed you as well." She hugged the animal. "We have a long way to travel. But don't worry. I won't make you walk the entire way."

That earned Meilin another lick from the Great Panda.

"We'll only have a few hours of travel before we have to stop," Meilin said to Anka. "Do you think there's any way we could travel during the day?"

"I don't think we can chance it," she said. "My powers can conceal us, but not when we're constantly moving. And certainly not over landscapes as open as this."

"Then we'd better get moving," Meilin said. "Everyone ready?"

Conor sat up from the ground. A few blades of grass poked from his blond hair. "Where's Abeke? Didn't she run off to get—?"

"Already back," Abeke said, holding up a rabbit. Uraza followed with another white rabbit between her jaws. "Hopefully we'll be able to hunt more along the way," she said. "It would be good to avoid any big settlements for as long as possible."

"We'll have to stop eventually," Conor said. "The closer we get to Trunswick, the colder the days will become." He nodded toward Rollan. "That is, unless Rollan shares his cloak with us."

Rollan seemed to blush as he pulled the thick brown cloak tightly around him. "Hey, get your own, wolf-boy."

Meilin rolled her eyes. "Let's get moving." She gave Jhi one last pat, then called her back into passive state. "Worthy, this is your territory," she said to the Red-cloak. "Lead the way."

They spent the next few nights traveling down dusty, rutted dirt roads and twisting paths while sleeping during daylight. Abeke and Conor were able to find food for them, but as Conor had suggested, food wasn't their major problem. It was cold during the day, and even more frigid at night. Rollan, now carrying the larger of the group's two packs, had eventually given up his brown cloak to others as they took turns sleeping. The first snow flurries had already begun to dust the landscape. They would need to stop soon for warmer clothes.

But it wasn't just snow that they encountered on their trek. Meilin also saw country cottages in shambles, dilapidated wooden fences along many of the roads, and the skeletons of burned bridges over small, winding streams. Sheep and pigs, once clearly domesticated, now ran wild, without a shepherd or farmer in sight to watch over them.

"What do you think happened here?" Anka asked a couple of days later as they paused by another abandoned, crumbling home. "Is all this destruction from the Second Devourer War? I thought they would have had a chance to rebuild by now."

"I'm going to scout on ahead," Conor said. "Maybe I can find some food. Or somewhere to bed down." Briggan nuzzled his partner's hand, then took off up the road. Conor, his ax tight in his hands, ran behind him.

Meilin placed her staff against the crumbling stone wall separating the house from the road. "This isn't the work of the Conquerors," she told Anka. "It was Greencloaks, when they were under the power of Zerif and the Wyrm."

"I only heard about the battles in Nilo and Stetriol," Anka said.

"They were everywhere," Meilin said. "The Wyrm wanted to control everything and everyone. And once it had the Greencloaks under its power, it had the perfect army. Mindless, powerful, trained warriors. And we were the heroes of the Second Devourer War. Every gate was already open to us."

"This wasn't the Greencloaks' fault," Abeke added, her voice huffy. "None of this would have happened if not for Zerif and the Wyrm. They alone are to blame for all this destruction." She cast her eyes at Conor up ahead.

"I know," Meilin said, keeping her voice calm. "I'm not accusing him."

Abeke sighed, and the tension released from her body. "I'm sorry. I know that you understand the truth." She looked up the road again. "I'm going to find Conor. You all catch up when you can."

"Should we follow them?" Rollan asked, once Abeke and Uraza had disappeared over a hill.

"No, give them a moment," Meilin said. She nodded toward Worthy, who was stretched out in the grass. "I don't think Worthy would mind a few extra minutes of rest."

Meilin took a sip of water from a canteen, then handed it to Anka. As soon as she took it, it turned a gray color to match the stones they sat against. "But as I understand it, Conor wasn't even in Greenhaven when Zerif attacked," Anka said.

Meilin nodded. She and Conor had been deep underground, in Sadre, when he finally succumbed to the Wyrm. She had seen it firsthand, how evil and destructive he'd become. "It doesn't matter where he was," Meilin said. "He still feels guilty about it. It wasn't his fault. He'll come to realize that, in time."

"How can you be so sure?" Anka asked.

Meilin didn't know how to answer Anka, so instead she began reorganizing her bag. According to Worthy, they were nearing a town. They needed supplies, so it would be a rare chance to indulge in some civilization. They could get some clothes. Food. And maybe a weapon or two.

Meilin stood, slipping her pack over her shoulders. "Rollan, want to wake Worthy?"

"More like Sleepy," Rollan said. "Seriously, how can he nap at a time like this?"

As Rollan walked to the Redcloak, who was now snoring, Meilin picked up a loose stone from the ground and returned it to the rock wall. Jhi could heal a lot of things, but unfortunately her powers couldn't fix this. "The people of Eura will eventually rebuild," she said. "Perhaps that's something we Greencloaks can help with, once we've found the three other gifts."

"You want to build houses and fences?" Anka asked. "That seems so unlike you. So . . . beneath you."

"Why? Because I'm a warrior?" Meilin shrugged. "I spent time helping to rebuild Zhong after the war. It's important work. Maybe even more important than always looking for a fight." She glanced at her quarter-staff. "Just because I'm good at battle doesn't mean I want to do it all the time. And if you hadn't noticed, I'm partnered with Jhi—a healer, not a fighter. Jhi helped me realize there's more to life than taking up arms every time there's a new threat." Meilin watched as Rollan tried to rouse Worthy, to little avail. The boy began sleepily pawing at Rollan's hands.

"So what will you do next, once this is over?" It took Meilin a second to realize that Anka was now standing beside her, instead of sitting down. "Retire your green cloak?"

"No way," she said. "I'll always be a Greencloak." She watched as Rollan tried to pull Worthy to his feet by his cloak. "Plus, I couldn't quit. Rollan would be lost without me."

"Yes, it's clear that you care for him very much," Anka replied.

"Yeah, he's okay." Meilin would have preferred to have Anka's chameleon powers right then. She hoped that it was too dark for the elder Greencloak to see how Meilin's skin was reddening.

"Not every Greencloak is best served on the battlefield," Anka said. "I wouldn't last five minutes in a real battle."

"Even the best warriors don't always return from battle," Meilin said. "That's just the way war works."

Meilin became quiet again as she envisioned the death of the Emperor of Zhong. She could still see the snarl of the hyena as it leaped past her. She could still see the emperor staggering, clutching his neck, and collapsing. Then the image morphed, and she was now watching her own father, General Teng, as he died on the battleground during the Second Devourer War. He and the emperor, both felled in similar ways. Both had died in silence, like true Zhongese warriors.

"Meilin? Are you okay?" Anka asked. "You became quiet all of a sudden."

"It's nothing. . . ." She looked at Anka, wishing she could see her face. She valued her friends, but she also enjoyed traveling with another person from Zhong. And a woman, no less.

"If you don't mind me asking," Meilin began. "What did your father say when you decided to join the Greencloaks?"

"He didn't know," Anka said. "He died in battle during the war, like General Teng."

Meilin hoped that her face didn't reveal how shocked she was. She hadn't told Anka who her father was. It still felt strange to talk about him out loud. In the past tense.

"I took up the cloak a few months afterward," Anka continued. "After everything the Greencloaks had done for Erdas—for Zhong—it seemed like the best way to help." She gave Meilin a wry smile. "Plus, it wasn't as if I could join the Zhongese army, could I?"

"I'll teach you some more fighting techniques when we make camp," Meilin said.

"That would be good, although I don't know how much help Toey will be in battle."

"I used to think the same about Jhi," Meilin said. "You'd be surprised by the different types of strength we draw from our partners when we fight." Then, a few moments later, she added. "How long have you known that General Teng was my father?"

"I've always known. You're a hero in Zhong, just like General Teng." Anka paused, and a few seconds later a small flash came before Meilin's eyes. Slowly, Anka's full form trickled into view, like spilled ink spreading across a blank page. Meilin realized the flash had been Anka calling Toey, her chameleon, into passive state.

"Just so you know, everyone in my village wept when we learned of General Teng's fate." Anka offered up a small, sympathetic smile. "The entire nation mourned. He was a true protector of Zhong."

Meilin turned from Anka then, so she wouldn't see her face. *Yep*, she thought, *I'd kill to have those chameleon powers right now.*

4

THE MARKET

"WHY CAN'T I GO?" WORTHY DEMANDED, CROSSING his arms and planting himself in front of Rollan and Anka. As he spoke, white tufts of cold air spilled from his mouth. His red cloak billowed behind him, making him look more ferocious than Rollan knew he really was.

"Really? You don't think that white mask will draw any attention?" Rollan asked. "We're supposed to be keeping a low profile. Blending in." According to Worthy and Conor, they were about five days away from Trunswick. Although unlikely, it was still possible that people from the village would recognize Conor and Worthy, which would jeopardize their mission.

"Don't you remember the last time you and Conor tried sneaking into a city?" Worthy said, still adamant. His words had as much bite as the frosty morning air. "If it wasn't for me, you would have been captured."

"Worthy, heroes aren't supposed to boast," Meilin said. "And don't worry—I'll be there to keep Rollan in line."

"Um, thanks for the vote of confidence," Rollan said as Meilin smirked at him. Then he nodded toward Conor. "Why can't you be more like Conor, Worthy? You don't see him complaining about staying at camp." A few feet away, Conor stomped out the remaining embers from their fire. They had used it to cook a snake that he and Briggan had caught last night. Worthy only took one bite before spitting out the tough, lean meat . . . which had just meant that there was more for Rollan to eat. Sure, Rollan liked to joke about how bad the food was when he was traveling, but it was almost always better than the food he'd had to forage from garbage bins while he was living on the streets in Concorba.

What will happen if the Greencloaks disband? he wondered. He knew he wouldn't have to go back to his old life as an orphan, but he was still worried. Would the Prime Minister force him to fight for Amaya? Force him to fight against his friends?

Force him to fight against Meilin?

He thought about his cloak, hidden in one of the packs now beside Conor. He had snuck it in there a few nights ago while the others were sleeping. Rollan had been the last of the four to take the Greencloak oath. Now he couldn't imagine being anything except a Greencloak. And he couldn't imagine giving up Tarik's cloak.

"What about Anka?" Worthy asked as she and Abeke approached them. He was still rambling on about accompanying them into the village. "She could turn me invisible."

Anka was shaking her head before Worthy even finished. "It's too hard for me to hide everyone when we're moving, especially in a crowded market," she said. Anka looked so different with her chameleon in passive state. Her hair was as black as Meilin's bangs, but much shorter. The jade bracelet on her wrist covered the mark of her spirit animal. "The second someone bumps into you, our cover will be blown," she continued. "How much attention do you think that will draw, once people realize there are invisible kids walking around the square?"

"Think of it this way," Rollan said, "you can catch up on your beauty sleep."

Worthy looked back toward their makeshift campsite. "Perhaps a small nap wouldn't be so bad. Have to be ready whenever the Oathbound show up. Just try to find some decent food. Something not so . . . slithery."

"We'll see what we can do," Abeke said. She knelt and petted Uraza. "Sorry, girl. I know you want to run free, but Rollan's right. We've got to blend in, and that's hard to do with a purple-eyed leopard walking around." With a growl, Uraza disappeared onto her arm. Abeke stood and looked at Rollan. "I won't lie. I'm pretty jealous of you and Essix right now."

Essix sat on a nearby branch, surveying the group. She hadn't liked their snake dinner, either, but Rollan was sure she was finding plenty to eat around the countryside. Essix had always been more of a free spirit, preferring to roam the skies instead of remaining hidden on Rollan's body. But even with him on the ground and her in the air, their bond was unshakable.

"Remember, we aren't supposed to know one another," Anka said to Rollan and Meilin, as she and

Abeke started down the road. "Don't talk to us unless you absolutely have to."

"See you there," Rollan said. "Or I guess, maybe not." They'd decided to split up that morning, in order to draw even less attention to themselves. Rollan and Meilin would approach the village from the west, while Abeke and Anka took a southern, circular route. Abeke and Anka were responsible for gathering clothes and food. Rollan had wanted to buy the food, but of course, Meilin wanted to be in charge of purchasing the weapons. Anka had offered to switch places with him, but he politely declined, turning bright red in the process.

"Worthy is right about one thing," Meilin said as Anka and Abeke disappeared around a bend. "We need to be ready whenever the Oathbound show up. I'm surprised we haven't seen any trace of them yet."

"Maybe they don't know we're here," Rollan said.

"Well, they weren't supposed to know we were in Amaya, and they were able to track us anyway," Meilin said. "I almost wish they'd show up already. Anything is better than all this sneaking around. If I have to fight, I prefer to face my enemies head-on."

"Patience, Your Highness," Rollan said. He knew how much it got underneath Meilin's skin when he called her things like that, which just made him tease her more. "What do you think, Essix? Want to take another look to see if you can spot those goons in black?"

Essix and Rollan held each other's gaze for a few seconds, then the Great Falcon took flight, her talons sharp and pointed, her feathers rustling in the breeze.

"Thanks," Meilin said. "Let's get moving."

They didn't speak for a while. Meilin may have liked all the silence, but Rollan thought the rolling countryside was *too* quiet. He missed the busy streets of Concorba. The crowded hallways in Greenhaven Castle. His mind tended to wander when he was surrounded by silence, and he often found himself thinking about things that he'd rather not. His mother. The Wyrm. Shane. Tarik.

Rollan knew he was acting childish—like a toddler refusing to give up his baby blanket. He was a Greencloak in spirit and heart—and he didn't need Tarik's cloak to remind him of his oath. Worse, as a kid growing up on the streets, he knew the dangers of getting too sentimental about material things. But even with all that—even with all the risks of getting caught—he just couldn't part with the cloak. Not yet. It was old, tattered, and faded, but it was all that he had to remind him of their former mentor. Rollan had been clutching that very cloak in his hands when Tarik was killed in battle. Part of Rollan feared that once it was gone, then Tarik would be truly gone as well.

"Are you okay?" Meilin asked. "You're frowning."

"Oh." Rollan shook his head, trying to clear those thoughts away. He plastered a smile on his face. "Was just thinking about all the yummy foods I'm going to try when we get to the market."

Meilin arched an eyebrow. She knew him too well. She wasn't buying it. "Tell me what you're really thinking about," she said. "Maybe it'll help to talk."

The sun had just broken the tree line, helping to drive the chill from the air. He noticed how the yellow-orange rays seemed to make Meilin's face glow.

Rollan shook his head. "I'll be okay, but thanks for asking."

They didn't speak for a few more moments. Rollan could sense Meilin looking at him, but he was too nervous to look back. Then he felt something tugging at his arm.

It was her hand, sliding into his.

Rollan was so surprised, he almost tripped over a rock. He caught himself before falling, then gave Meilin's hand a slight squeeze. "Did you see that big boulder?" he asked. "It was huge. Colossal. Mountain-sized." He stood a little taller. "You'd better stick close to me, just in case we see any other dangerous obstacles in our way."

She rolled her eyes, but she didn't let go of his hand.

Green fields stretched as far as Rollan could see. Without sheep and goats to graze the land, many of the fields were overgrown with long, flowing blades of grass. In others, thorny wildflowers and weeds threatened to overtake the lush meadows. Ahead on a hill, a few sheep wandered in a pasture, the fence weathered but holding. A young boy stood with a crook and a small dog at his side. Rollan was glad to see the boy. It proved that not everything had been destroyed. Farther away, plumes of black smoke rose to the sky. It was probably from the bakers and cooks in the village, preparing their wares for the day's shoppers. *A warm loaf of bread would be nice*, he thought to himself. He was sure that Essix would enjoy it as well.

"So what do you think about Worthy?" Meilin asked after a few more moments. "Do you trust him yet?"

Rollan wanted to keep the imaginary taste of warm rolls and honey in his head for a little bit longer, but it was already fading away. "What makes you ask that?"

She tugged on Rollan's arm. "You can be a little mean to him sometimes."

Meilin was way too perceptive. He sighed. "I'm trying to like him," Rollan said. "But I don't know if I'll ever really trust a Redcloak."

"But they helped us defeat the Wyrm. And we wouldn't have gotten away from the Oathbound in Amaya if not for them."

"Yeah, but they were Conquerors before they were Redcloacks," Rollan said. "Remember Shane—before he turned into a Redcloak? How he betrayed us at Greenhaven Castle? Remember how he and the other Conquerors tricked my mom into taking the Bile so they could control her? How they forced her to attack me? Remember what happened to your father? To Tarik?" His voice caught when mentioning his former mentor's name. "They have a lot to prove before they're ready to be the 'next protectors of Erdas.' For all we know, they might be planning to stab us in the back and steal the gifts as soon as we collect them all." As Rollan said this, he realized that he had left the Heart of the Land, the gift from Amaya, at the campsite for safekeeping. Now he wondered if that had been a good idea.

Meilin stared ahead; she seemed to be considering Rollan's argument. The Meilin of old would have been arguing back before Rollan had even finished talking, but she'd changed a lot since he'd first met her. She was calmer now. More thoughtful. More considerate. A lot like Jhi.

Of course, they all had changed a bunch since they'd first become a team. That's what happened when you risked your life to save the world from total destruction. Twice.

"Okay, I understand where you're coming from," she said slowly. "Really, I do. But what if you try to separate Worthy from all the other Redcloaks. *He's* not so bad, right?"

Rollan shrugged. "I know he's been a big help here of late, but that still doesn't erase all the bad things he did when he was plain old Devin Trunswick. Don't forget, he and I didn't exactly hit it off the first time we met."

Meilin smirked. "Are you still mad about him jailing you in the Howling House? Didn't he apologize to you on the boat on the way here?"

"You'd still be mad, too, if you'd seen the size of those rats in that little cell. And the smell—it was worse than a pigsty." He ran his thumb across the back of her hand, tickling her. "There were spiders, too. Thousands of them, all with red eyes and hairy legs and—"

"Okay, I get your point," Meilin said, shuddering. With her free hand, she loosened the scarf covering her neck. "But that was a long time ago. Essix seems to like Worthy."

"She just likes to hang around him because he always has leftover food," Rollan said. "What do *you* think about him?"

"I *want* to trust him," she said. "He's different now, and I'm not just talking about his wildcat powers. He really wants to do good."

"Good is relative," he said. "Think about it—I'm sure that the Emperor of Zhong and the Prime Minister of Amaya thought they were acting in their lands' best interests when they told the Greencloaks to disband. They were doing what was good for their people."

"But not what was good for Erdas."

Rollan shrugged. "Again, it's all in the eye of the beholder." The dark plumes of smoke from the village market were getting larger. They would reach the town soon. Rollan almost wished it were farther away. That wouldn't have been so bad . . . as long as he got to hold Meilin's hand for the rest of the walk. That would have made the extra distance totally worthwhile.

"What about Anka?" Rollan asked. "I saw you training her yesterday in camp."

"I like her. It's nice to have someone from Zhong around," she said. "We have a lot in common."

"You mean you're both afraid of spiders?" Rollan teased.

"I'm not afraid of spiders," Meilin said. "I'm—what is it?"

Rollan had stopped walking. He let go of Meilin's hand and turned his face to the sky. "It's Essix. She's calling me." He looked around to make sure they were alone on the path. "Watch my back."

She nodded, rolling up her sleeves. When Rollan saw through Essix's eyes, it was almost like he was in a trance; in a slumber from which he sometimes couldn't easily wake himself. He wouldn't be able to defend himself if someone attacked while he was floating around in the falcon's head. That was a benefit of having Meilin around. Even without weapons, her fists and feet were just as deadly as swords and staves.

Rollan closed his eyes. His world fell away—his fingers and toes, the chill from the morning air, the warmth he'd just experienced by holding Meilin's hand—and he suddenly felt a whoosh as he connected with Essix. Clouds floated ahead. For a second, Rollan wondered if the bird was just trying to show off her fancy flying skills. Then Essix dove, and the market square rushed up to him. Rollan knew he was probably staggering; he always got a little motion sickness when she flew too fast. Essix eventually leveled out and soared to the top of a lush evergreen tree. Rollan used her eyes to search the already-bustling crowd. For a small village market, it was filled to capacity with merchants and shoppers. Burlap tents sat in a grid, with merchants shouting out their deals to anyone within earshot. Each baker boasted of having the best sweets in the village; each tailor promised that he sold the finest clothes and warmest coats. Woman wearing plain, long skirts and scarves over their heads walked through the square, using their slender fingers to judge the craftsmanship of the wool quilts and thick winter hats. Their small children lagged behind, asking for coins to buy a piece of hard candy or a muffin or a scone. A few steps away, less well-to-do kids stood on the outskirts of the market, hoping on strangers' kindness for their next meals. Rollan focused on the smallest child, a boy with a dirt-streaked face and a faded blue blanket draped around his bony shoulders. Rollan tried to memorize the boy's face. If Rollan could find them again, he'd buy something for the kids when he reached the village. That had been him, before becoming a Greencloak.

He kept searching the grounds. Essix had obviously seen something, but he didn't know what. Finally, he saw it. Or rather, them. Three men and a woman in black uniforms, with brass wrist protectors and neck collars, stepped out of a tent.

The Oathbound were in Eura.

Rollan watched as the men followed the woman to another tent. The woman was tall, with broad shoulders and a long brown braid. The merchant stepped toward them, no doubt trying to sell his latest, overpriced goods. The woman held up a parchment, cutting him off mid-sales pitch. She jutted her finger at the document while the merchant shook his head. Then the woman leaned in and whispered something else. The man's eyes widened, and his mouth became slack-jawed. The woman, now smirking, patted the man on the cheek–not at all an affectionate touch–then moved on to the next tent. The merchant remained in place, rubbing his face. Rollan wasn't sure, but it looked like the woman had drawn blood.

After the Oathbound disappeared into another tent, Essix took off from her perch. Rollan understood exactly where the falcon was off to. She would find Anka and Abeke, while Rollan and Meilin rushed to the market.

The bird's view of the sky faded away. Rollan blinked. He was back on the roadside with Meilin. "What's wrong?" she asked.

"Oathbound." He took her hand again. "Come on. We need to find the others."

Rollan and Meilin had to stop running once they drew closer to the market. Their narrow path had merged with a larger road bustling with travelers on foot and horseback. Rollan wished Conor was here to see all the people heading to the village. It was another sign that Eura was rebuilding. Things were getting better.

Rollan and Meilin slipped into the stream of travelers and entered the village. A horse carrying a large, lopsided pack on its back huffed in his direction, blowing stale air across his face. Rollan shook his fist at the animal. He still didn't like horses. The feeling was seemingly mutual.

Nearing the market at the center of the village, Rollin heard a squawk. Essix! She sat in another tree, almost hidden by its thick, knobby branches. She and Rollan stared at each other, and she quickly made a flapping motion with her brown wings.

"She wants us to follow her," Rollan said. "I think she found them."

The bird took flight. Meilin and Rollan followed a few steps behind, both glancing in opposite directions, trying to keep an eye out for the Oathbound. Rollan had seen only four of them in the market—a number that didn't pose too much of a threat—but they may have been Marked, making a potential battle even more of a challenge. Others were likely camped nearby. They'd faced off against a full garrison in Amaya. He didn't expect anything different here.

As he passed a wooden cart, a familiar flash of faded blue cloth caught Rollan's eye. He paused, then turned away from the market.

"Rollan," Meilin whispered. "Where are you going?"

Rollan kept walking toward the boy. He and a few other kids stood between two carts, either using them to hide or perhaps to protect themselves from the biting wind. Rollan checked his pockets. He could only spare a few coins. It wasn't much, but it would have to do.

"Don't spend them all in one place," he said, tossing two coins to the boy. "And share with your friends."

The boy gave Rollan a smile warm enough to melt the coldest of hearts. Rollan returned to Meilin. She was grinning as well.

"You're such a softie," she said. "It's one of my favorite things about you." Then her smile faded. "But we should hurry. For all we know, the Oathbound have already found Anka and Abeke."

Rollan looked at the sky. Essix circled over a large white-and-brown tent. A woman in a stained apron stood in front, showing off slabs of dried meats.

Rollan's stomach grumbled. That looked so much better than snake stew.

They picked up the pace, weaving through villagers. They entered the tent to find Abeke and Anka quarreling with a merchant. It seemed to be over the price of a bag of grain.

Abeke was always astute about her surroundings, even when Uraza was in passive state. She stopped arguing with the man, turned, and caught sight of Rollan and Meilin. She whispered something to Anka.

Not looking in their direction, Anka slowly nodded, then continued her talk with the merchant.

Abeke walked toward them, under the pretense of looking at other provisions on the makeshift shelves.

"What are you doing here?" Abeke didn't look at Rollan as she whispered. "Anka said—"

"We caught sight of the Oathbound," Rollan replied. "They're here, in the village."

Abeke drew a long breath, then nodded. "I was afraid you'd say that. I've been uneasy ever since we reached the village." She picked up a jar of spiced peaches, then frowned at them. "We picked up some warm clothes and are almost finished with the food. You two should head back to the camp. We'll meet you there as soon as we can."

"I don't think that's a good idea," Rollan said. "If there are Oathbound here, we'll have a better chance of defeating them together."

"Yes, but I'd rather not see them at all," Abeke said. She chanced a glance at Meilin. "What do you think?"

"I think if they're here, in Eura, then we'll have to fight them sooner or later," Meilin said. "And I think it would be easier if we faced them with better weapons."

"You want to buy a sword, don't you?" Rollan said. "How many arrows do you have left, Abeke?"

"Not nearly enough." Abeke had been collecting rocks to shape into arrowheads during their trek through Eura, but it was difficult to see them at night. "There's a trading post on the west side of the market— the tent with the maroon flag. It's probably the best place for you to find weapons. Anka and I will finish up here and meet you back at camp."

They nodded, then slipped back out of the tent. The trading post wasn't hard to find. In addition to the maroon flag waving overhead, it was surrounded by trappers and hunters. They stood outside, laughing and singing.

Meilin frowned as she passed the men. "You said your cell at the Howling House smelled like a pigsty. Was it as wretched as these men smell?" she asked, almost gagging.

Rollan had put his hand over his nose. "These guys are way worse. Maybe that's how they attract their prey—by imitating the scent of dead animals."

Once in the tent, they quickly made their way toward the weapons. The selection was meager—swords made from rusted steel and bows from flimsy wood—but they were able to find a couple quivers of arrows for Abeke.

"What can I help you kids with?" a woman asked, approaching them. Her apron matched the flag flying over the tent. The wart on the end of her nose was large enough to be its own body part.

"Just these," Meilin said, holding up the arrows. "That is, unless you have any decent swords."

"Something just came in." She patted her graying hair, rolled up tightly into a bun. "Come. Take a look. I'll give you a good price."

They followed the woman to the center of the tent. Behind them, about twenty hunters entered. They were loud, their drinks sloshing from their mugs as they lumbered through the post.

The woman took a sword from behind the counter. She slowly removed it from the black leather scabbard. It was a beautiful, single-edged blade, clearly cared for. There didn't seem to be a single nick in the metal. The hilt also looked new, with intricate symbols carved into the steel.

"It's a falchion," the merchant said. "One of the trappers just brought it in for a trade."

"I'm familiar," Meilin said. "It's similar to the Zhongese dao." She picked up the sword, then considered its weight. She took a few steps away, quickly spinning the weapon in her hands. The blade almost buzzed as it sliced the air.

"It's a good weapon," Meilin finally said. "It's well-balanced."

The merchant studied Meilin. "You're pretty good with a sword. Most of the hunters swing it like an ax, but you . . . you've been trained in proper swordplay technique." She scratched her nose. "What did you say your name was again? And what brings you to this little village?"

Meilin stiffened ever so slightly. Rollan realized that she might have been *too* good with the weapon.

"My father used to be a warrior. He trained me." She quickly returned the sword back to the counter. "But I gave that up. Too messy. Now I just sing and dance." She looped her arm into Rollan's and smiled broadly. "We're traveling performers."

"Did someone say performers?"

Rollan turned. The group of trappers must have overheard their conversation. Each carried a long, two-sided ax, similar to Conor's. Their fur boots were caked with mud.

At least Rollan hoped it was mud.

The largest of them, a bearded man with a belly shaped like a big black cauldron, stumbled forward. "How about you all put on a little performance? After weeks in the wilds, my mates and I could use a good show."

Rollan quickly sized up the men. About half of them had encircled Rollan and Meilin. That meant at least ten more were roaming around inside the tent, and no telling how many remained *outside*. He was sure that he and Meilin could get away, but a dramatic escape would draw too much attention. The Oathbound soldiers were probably still in the market.

"Well?" the trapper asked, scratching at his red-and-gray beard. Flakes of dandruff fell to the ground. "You going to perform for us or not? Or are you not any good?"

Meilin let go of Rollan's arm. "If you insist," she said. "I just hope you all tip well."

Meilin unwrapped her scarf from her neck as she moved to the center of the group. Rollan slowly moved his hand toward his dagger. He wanted to be ready whenever she gave the signal.

But Meilin didn't take a fighting stance. Instead, she closed her eyes and placed her hands in front of her like she was meditating. Slowly she balanced on one foot. And then she tipped to her toes and began to spin like a top. Exiting her spin, she leaped through the air, her arms wide, the scarf twirling around her like a silk ribbon. She followed that up with three backflips.

Rollan couldn't believe it. She was actually dancing.

The trappers began to clap and cheer. Meilin began to move faster, performing more spins, and flipping even higher. Her scarf was like an extension of her, twisting whenever she twisted, spinning whenever she spun.

Something hit Rollan against the back of his head. He turned, ready to fight . . . and then he saw the gold coin on the ground.

Cupping his hands, he began collecting money from the men. They were generous—both of Rollan's pockets were weighted down with gold and silver pieces once Meilin had finished her routine. As she took her last bows, Rollan realized that she hadn't even broken a sweat.

"Let's get those arrows and get out of here," he said, dumping the money into her hands. More trappers had entered the shop. They seemed friendly enough, but he didn't want to press his luck.

Her eyes widened as she counted the money. "I think there's enough here to buy both quivers *and* the sword."

"Meilin, you already have a weapon. Or do you not remember the quarterstaff that you swindled from that pirate on the boat?"

"I didn't swindle him," Meilin said. "I won that arm-wrestling contest fair and square. The rules didn't specify that we couldn't use a spirit animal." She glanced at the merchant. She had laid the sword out on the counter, along with two quivers of arrows. "Maybe she'll negotiate," she said.

"Just hurry up and—"

"Jolly good show, mates," the large trapper said, interrupting them. He had particularly seemed to enjoy the dance, clapping and doing a jig during Meilin's performance. His belly had looked like it was moving in slow motion. "So what do *you* do?" he asked, slapping Rollan on the back.

"I'm a dancer in training," Rollan said, rubbing his shoulder blade. Then he smiled. "Actually, more like the company jester."

Rollan had been in enough situations to know that when lying, it was best to tell the truth as much as possible.

"So where are you kids off to next?" he asked. "I'll be back in the wild with my mates soon, and it would be nice to see a proper performance."

"Um . . . why don't you go ahead and finish getting those supplies," Rollan said to Meilin. He couldn't tell if the trapper was really interested in their show, or if he was trying to out-bluff Rollan. Either way, Rollan knew they needed to make a quick exit.

Meilin nodded and headed to the counter.

"Yeah, you should totally check out one of our shows," Rollan said to the man. "I'm not sure where we're off to next. Like I said, I'm new to the group. They don't tell me anything—just where to sleep and when to rise. The real brains of our troupe is still in camp, off the road to the west of town."

They had actually bedded down to the east of town. Just in case his ploy didn't work, he hoped the trapper would search there instead of their real location.

"Well, where have you been to?" he asked.

"We passed through Betarvius a few days ago," Rollan said. Other than Trunswick, it was the only name of a town that he remembered. They hadn't stopped there, but he had seen signs for it along the trail.

"Oh, is that so?" The trapper's eyes creased, and Rollan's mouth went dry. Did the trapper know that Rollan was lying? Had Rollan said something to tip him off? That was the problem with bluffing too much. Lie enough times and you're eventually going to get caught.

"Did you try the pickled hog toes?" the trapper continued, scratching his thick beard. He took a lumbering step toward Rollan. "The town is famous for them."

"No, um, I'm more of a vegetarian," Rollan said. "I'd better get my friend. Nice talking to you."

Rollan rushed to the counter. "Look, I'm trying to be reasonable," Meilin was saying to the merchant. "But there is no way I'm paying that much for that sword. Perhaps you could—"

"We're good with just the arrows," Rollan said, picking up the quivers. "Thanks." He grabbed Meilin's hand and pulled her out of the tent.

"I just needed a few more minutes," she said. "I almost had her talked down."

"We didn't have a few more minutes," Rollan said. He pulled Meilin into a narrow space between two tents and waited. Sure enough, the large trapper stormed by, with two other men following him.

"Trouble?" she asked.

"Maybe. The trapper was asking too many questions. I tried to throw him off our trail. We'll see if it worked." Then he smiled. "You were awesome back there, by the way. Why don't you dance like that more often?"

She shrugged. "Dancing and fighting aren't all that

different." She looked over her shoulder, back at the tent, and sighed.

"Don't worry," Rollan said. "I'm sure we'll be able to make it out of the village without being caught."

"Oh, it's not that," she said. "I was just thinking—that was a really nice sword."

REMEMBERING
OLD FRIENDS

ABEKE RELEASED URAZA AS SOON AS THEY WERE within view of their campsite. She had told Anka that she wanted Uraza alert and ready, just in case any Oathbound soldiers were nearby. But if she was being honest, she also wanted Uraza by her side because she hated the idea of not seeing—and not sensing—her animal partner.

Abeke's stomach twisted into a knot and her mouth went coppery every time she relived the memory when Uraza had been stolen from her. How she'd gone from sharing her every thought with the leopard to suddenly feeling nothing. It was like falling endlessly down a dark, deep, cold pit. She hadn't known what loneliness truly felt like until their bond was ripped apart.

But that sense of loneliness paled in comparison to how Abeke had felt when she'd actually *fought* Uraza. The leopard, while under Zerif's control, had tried to attack her. Abeke was sure that her spirit animal would have killed her, if not for Shane. He'd put himself between Abeke and the Great Beast, screaming in pain as the golden leopard sank her teeth into him and shook him like an empty burlap sack. Abeke had been forced to fire on Uraza, shooting her in the leg in order to get her to release Shane, but it had been too late. Shane was gone.

Abeke often found herself looking at Uraza's hind right leg when she thought the animal was asleep. She couldn't see the results of the wound from her arrow— Uraza's golden fur had covered any resulting scar. But still, she knew it was there, hidden out of sight. A wound dealt by her own hand.

Uraza, perhaps sensing what was going through Abeke's mind, lovingly rubbed against her leg. Abeke knelt and scratched the leopard behind the ears. Abeke had been surprised, and even comforted, by the amount of affection that they'd shown each other since rebonding.

She often wondered how Uraza had felt when their bond had been snapped. Did she feel the pain as well? The emptiness? And how had the leopard felt under Zerif's control? Did she know what she was doing when she attacked Shane? When she tried to attack Abeke?

Perhaps they both needed comfort.

As they waited for the sun to set, Anka suggested they all rest, but that seemed impossible with the threat of the Oathbound looming over them. Meilin had told the others how she and Rollan tried to throw the villagers off their trail. No one really trusted that it would work.

Finally, after the sun dipped below the tree line, they packed up and continued their journey toward

Trunswick. Worthy and Abeke took the lead, taking the group through an overgrown, lush forest. Large pine trees reached to the sky, blocking what little light they received from the moon. Abeke winced as pine-cones and needles crunched underfoot—they were sure to draw the attention of the Oathbound.

Worthy eventually directed them to a small, barely noticeable trail snaking through the trees. In some places, the path was so narrow that they couldn't walk side by side. In other places, tree branches and exposed roots had overtaken the trail, slowing their travel considerably. However, this route was safer than taking one of the roads, now that they knew the Oathbound had reached Eura.

Even with Uraza boosting her senses, it was hard for Abeke to see in the forest. Every snap of a twig, every howl of an animal, every caw of a bird put Abeke on edge. It was like the forest itself were looking down on them, watching and waiting to pounce.

"Look sharp," Abeke said to Uraza. "They could be anywhere."

"No way they'll find us here," Worthy said, ducking underneath a low branch. "No one knows about this path." He glanced at Abeke, his slitted eyes stark beneath his white mask. "You move like Uraza, you know. Delicately. Softly. All catlike."

"So do you."

Worthy leaped and did a flip, just to show off. He landed in a crouch, on top of a stump. "Yep. It's one of the only benefits of merging with my spirit animal."

Abeke could have shown off as well, and probably could have leaped even higher than Worthy had, but that didn't seem like such a good idea. "Maybe you should save your energy for our enemy," Abeke offered.

Worthy just nodded. They continued on in silence for a few more paces, now walking shoulder to shoulder. Behind her, Abeke heard Rollan and Meilin arguing over her dance moves. Apparently, Rollan was challenging her to a dance-off once they saved the world—again. Farther behind them were Conor and Briggan, guarding the rear. Like Abeke, Conor seemed to be so much more at peace with his spirit animal at his side, not stuck in passive state. Anka was somewhere in the group as well, but it was hard for Abeke to sense her, especially when she was using her chameleon powers.

They reached a small river cutting through the forest. The bubbling of the water was nice. Calming. Abeke could imagine living in a place like this. Disappearing from the world.

They stopped to take a sip of water. She cupped her hands into the cool river, then brought the water to her mouth.

Uraza knelt beside Abeke and stuck her snout close to the water, doing her best to reach the river without getting her paws muddy. She quickly lapped it up with her tongue, causing small waves of water to ripple away from her. Uraza paused, and her eyes narrowed.

"What is it?" Abeke asked. "Do you hear something?"

Uraza nodded toward the water. There, below the surface, swam three large fish.

"Not today," Abeke said, running her hands along

the animal's black-and-gold fur. Water from Abeke's hands beaded on her coat. Then, before the cat could respond, Abeke cupped her hand in the water and splashed Uraza. The leopard jumped and yowled. Then she playfully tackled Abeke, nipping at her ears and fingers.

"I'm sorry!" Abeke laughed, hugging Uraza around the neck. "I know you don't like the water. I just couldn't help myself."

She turned around. Worthy sat on a log behind her. She wondered if he'd been watching her the entire time.

"I could never understand what he saw in you," Worthy said. "I thought you all were just self-righteous brats. But now that I've spent some time with you, I can see why he liked you so much."

Abeke didn't need to ask who *he* was. She rose from the river, wiping her hands on her clothes. "What is this river called?" she asked, trying to change the subject.

"I believe this is a small tributary of the Adunder, one of the widest and longest rivers in Eura," Worthy said. "It starts at the Petral Mountains and continues all the way to the coast." He hopped from his log and took a drink of water as well. Abeke noticed that he drank it like Uraza, on all fours with his face close to the water.

He stood and wiped his face. "Want me to knock down a tree for us to use as a bridge?"

Abeke smiled. "No, I have a better idea. Come on, Uraza." Abeke and the Great Leopard backed up from the river, then exploded down the trail. Abeke felt the leopard's power flowing between them. Her legs felt stronger, her steps surer. She resisted the urge to roar as she planted her foot and took off in a leap across the water, her limbs spinning in the air. Uraza was right beside her, the leopard's body long and sleek in the nighttime sky. They landed together, their feet clearing the muddy banks. They turned to see Worthy on the other side. Slowly, he clapped his hands.

"Do you want *us* to cut down a tree for *you*?" Abeke asked.

He shook his head. "I'll find my own way across." Dropping into a squat, he lunged for the nearest tree. His claws sank into the dark wood as he moved higher into the air. He then leaped onto a nearby branch. Thin and wiry, it looked too small to hold his weight. But Abeke quickly realized what Worthy was doing. Using the branch like a rope, he swung from tree to tree, his cloak billowing behind him as he crossed the river.

He performed a triple somersault before landing beside Abeke. She rolled her eyes, but still clapped for him.

"Shane also mentioned you were a great acrobat," he said.

Abeke sighed. *Maybe it would be good to talk about him*, she told herself. She often wanted to, but always felt uncomfortable when bringing him up around the other Greencloaks. She had forgiven him for betraying them, but the others had not. And in Rollan's case, she didn't know if he would ever forgive Shane.

"Did Shane really talk about me?" she asked. Even though they were alone, she found herself whispering.

"Sometimes," Worthy said. "You know, since we're being honest and all, most of us Redcloaks didn't really like you guys at first. Nobody likes being beat, even if they eventually realize they're fighting on the wrong side." They started walking again, but more slowly. "Shane would let us joke around about the Greencloaks, even letting us say some not-so-nice things about Conor and Rollan. Especially Rollan. But you were always off-limits."

Abeke didn't know how to respond. There was so little that she knew about Shane once he'd become the leader of the Redcloaks. He had become this whole new person—someone capable of redeeming himself for his past actions. But now he was gone.

"Shane—or King, as we called him—was a good leader," Worthy continued. "Without him, there's no telling what any of us Redcloaks would be doing right now. I'd probably be locked in a cage in someone's sideshow carnival."

Abeke laughed. "Somehow, I don't see you staying locked up for very long. You're a very good fighter."

Abeke could see Worthy stand straighter at that remark. "Thanks. I wish I could say it was all my natural and self-taught abilities, but King also trained us. Better than Zerif ever did. He turned us into a real fighting force. A team. He showed us how to work together."

Abeke narrowed her eyes and really considered Worthy for a few moments. In the dark, with the red cloak billowing around his shoulders, he almost looked like Shane.

Worthy coughed and looked away. "What? Do I have something stuck to my mask?"

"You miss him, don't you?" she said. "You miss Shane."

He nodded after a few seconds of silence. "Yeah. I guess I do."

She placed her hand on his shoulder. "You know you can talk to me about him anytime." She shrugged. "I miss him, too. It might be good for me as well."

"You were there when he . . ." Worthy glanced at Uraza, then back at Abeke. "You were there at the end, right? Was he in a lot of pain?"

"He didn't suffer long," Abeke said.

"Look, I know you and he were . . . close," he said. "And I know how he died. Uraza—"

"She didn't kill him," Abeke said, a tremble in her voice. Her hands had instinctively balled into fists. "It wasn't Uraza's fault."

"Yeah. I know," Worthy said. "It was really Zerif and the Wyrm that were forcing her to do it, but still, and the end, it was *her* teeth pressed into his flesh." He pulled at his collar. "I guess what I'm asking is—given how you felt about him—are you ever angry at Uraza?"

"Of course not," Abeke said as she stopped walking. She reminded herself to calm down. Worthy wasn't the enemy. None of them were. "Remember how, because of the Bile, you were forced to do a lot of things against your will?" After he nodded, she said, "Uraza was the same way. So was Conor. So were all the Greencloaks." They began walking again. "However, that doesn't mean I'm not sad about what happened between us. I wish Zerif had never stolen her. I wish I didn't have to shoot her in the leg. But those things happened whether she or I like them or not. And now we just have to figure out a way to live with our actions."

But as Abeke spoke, she realized she didn't know if Uraza had forgiven *her* for shooting her with an arrow.

Uraza hadn't had a choice in the matter when attacking Shane. Abeke had. Abeke had willingly chosen to harm her partner.

"You know, I've never admitted this," Worthy began, "but I talk to Elda like she's still here."

"Elda?"

"My wildcat." He looked around, like he was making sure that no one was close enough to hear them. "I talk to her sometimes. In my head. I apologize for how I treated her. I made her do things against her will—kind of like what Gerathon did to me and the others that took the Bile."

Abeke remembered Worthy's wildcat. She was large and ferocious, with fur as black as squid ink. Her eyes had been golden, like Worthy's were now. She wasn't a natural spirit animal. She had been enslaved by the Bile. When drank by a human, the liquid could force a spirit animal bond, making the chosen animals smarter and more deadly—but also completely obedient. And when animals had drank the Bile, well . . . Abeke didn't wish that fate on the worst of her enemies.

"I did a lot of bad things, but now I finally have the chance to make things right," Worthy said. "Even if it takes the rest of my life, I'm going to make it up to the world. I'm going to redeem myself."

Abeke knew that Shane had felt the same way. And he *had* eventually redeemed himself.

At the cost of his life.

They continued on through the night. Worthy was actually a half-decent traveling companion when he wasn't complaining or whining.

Eventually they stopped for a longer break. "How much farther?" Worthy asked. "My legs are as soft as noodles."

Seeing the exhausted stoop of Worthy's posture made Abeke realize how tired she was as well. "Just a couple more hours," she said. "Then we'll look for somewhere to bed down. Take a rest until nightfall." She sat down on an overturned, partially buried log and took a sip of water. After a long drink, she offered the canteen to Worthy. As he finished off the water, Uraza nudged at the log, perhaps looking for some small vermin for a late-night snack.

"Knowing Meilin, she'll want to keep moving," Worthy said. He looked up at the canopy of tree branches, still blocking most of the moonlight from entering the forest. "She'll say this forest is dense enough that we can keep moving without being seen."

Abeke took the empty canteen from him. "You're probably right. But let's discuss it when the others catch up." Abeke could just see them approaching. It was hard to tell, but it almost looked like Rollan and Meilin were holding hands.

Worthy pulled a stick of jerky from his pocket. Breaking it into three pieces, he offered some to Uraza and Abeke. "I'm excited about going home," he said between bites. "A soft bed. Clean sheets. Maybe a warm meal or two—something other than snake and rabbit." He popped the last of the jerky into his mouth. "But I also really want to see my brother. I miss him." Worthy cleared his throat and gave Abeke a wayward glance. "But, um, don't tell Dawson I said that. I have a reputation to protect, after all."

"Don't worry," she said. "Your secret is safe with me."

He seemed to hesitate, then sat down beside Abeke. "Speaking of secrets, there's something I need to tell you. Something about the Wildcat's Claw." He took a deep breath. "I don't exactly know—"

"Wait." She placed her hand on his shoulder, quieting him. "Do you hear that?" she whispered.

"What is it?" Worthy asked, spinning around. "I don't hear anything."

"Yes. And that's the problem." The forest had suddenly grown too quiet. It was as if something had driven all the wildlife away.

Abeke slipped her bow from her shoulder and motioned for Worthy to follow her. They crept behind a large trunk and sank to the ground. Uraza crouched beside her.

"Uraza, go warn the others," Abeke said, staring into the leopard's purple eyes. "Lead them back to us. But quietly. Try to stay hidden as much as you can."

Uraza's tail flicked behind her and she sank even lower, then she took off through the forest. Her padded paws hardly made a sound as she scurried around the trees.

Abeke pulled an arrow from the new set of quivers Rollan and Meilin had purchased from the market. She was appreciative of the arrows, but she almost wished she'd just made more herself. Many of the new arrowheads were chipped and unbalanced, which could throw them off their mark when released.

She spun as she heard crunching leaves to her left. Nocking an arrow and pulling back on the string, she searched the darkness, looking for her target. Beside her, Worthy flexed his claws, uttering a low, guttural growl.

"Whoa! It's us," Anka whispered. A few seconds later, she and the others appeared in front of them. "Sorry."

"That was close," Abeke said, releasing the tension in her bow.

"Briggan and I sensed something, too," Conor said. He shrugged off the smaller of their two packs, then dropped down beside Abeke. "It feels like a trap."

"Do you think it could be the Oathbound?" Abeke asked.

"If so, they must have been following us," Worthy said. "This is one of the most hidden, most secret—what's that sound?"

Abeke heard it, too. A low whistling sound pierced the air. Suddenly recognizing it, she yelled, "Get down!"

They all dropped to the ground as an arrow flew overhead and lodged into a tree trunk. Two more arrows followed, each striking to the left and right of the group.

They scurried behind a log as more arrows sliced the night sky. "Look alive, Greencloaks," Abeke said, reloading her bow. "We're under attack."

TRAPPER ATTACK

MEILIN USUALLY LIKED THE THRILL OF HAND-TO-hand combat over the use of projectile weapons, but when an unseen enemy was firing arrows at her, she really wished she was a better archer.

"Can anyone see them?" Abeke asked, once the first flurry had ended. She quickly peeked over the log and fired in the direction of their attackers, but nothing seemed to connect. "I don't want to waste my arrows."

"We need to keep moving," Worthy said, his claws bared, ready to strike once given the opportunity. "We're sitting ducks out here."

"What do you think, Anka?" Conor said. "Can you hide us all with your chameleon's powers?"

It took Meilin a moment to realize the woman was shaking her head. "It would be possible . . . but we would have to move very slowly. It doesn't work if we're zigzagging around the forest, trying to take cover."

"Let's just slow down for a moment." Meilin braced herself against her quarterstaff. "It would be good to know what we're up against before we make our next move."

"You know, I would usually agree with you," Rollan said. "But not when people are shooting at us."

"We're fine for the time being," Meilin said as she considered their surroundings. They seemed to have pretty good cover thanks to the large overturned log and the dense trees surrounding them, but they were also pinned down, making it impossible for them to escape. The arrows seemed to be coming from directly ahead. She tried spying through the foliage, hoping to catch sight of the black uniforms or metallic neck and wrist braces of the Oathbound, but all she saw was green leaves and brown trees.

Meilin ducked as another arrow landed high above them. She closed her eyes and counted as others fired all around them. "There are at least eight archers."

"Eight Oathbound? That's not so bad," Conor said. "Better than that whole army we faced in Amaya." Briggan sat by his side, growling toward their unseen attackers. The wolf, like Meilin, preferred more direct combat as well.

"I don't think we're up against the Oathbound," Meilin said. She glanced at the arrow stuck in a tree above them. "Doesn't that look familiar?"

They all looked up, then at the matching arrow nocked in Abeke's bow. "It's the same arrows from the village!" Rollan said. "Do you think it's the trappers?"

Worthy nodded. "You know, that makes sense. They're the only people around here that would know this forest well. They'd know exactly where to hide in order to ambush us."

"I was afraid this would happen," Rollan said with a sigh. "One of the trappers started questioning me.

Asking me about where we'd traveled. I finally told him that we passed through Betarvius—"

Conor and Worthy groaned. Meilin wasn't sure, but it even looked like Briggan rolled his eyes.

"Yep, that was a mistake," Worthy finally said. "That place is a ghost town. Completely empty." He elbowed Rollan. "See, none of this would have happened if you'd taken me."

"Enough, Worthy," Conor snapped. "It was an honest mistake. How was he supposed to know . . ."

Conor stopped talking, shifting his body so he was turned away from the others. Meilin looked from Conor to Worthy. There was something else they knew—something more about the village—but neither seemed to want to continue talking.

"Look on the bright side," Rollan finally said. "At least it's not the Oathbound out there trying to kill us." They watched as another arrow soared overhead, settling in the brush far behind them. "These guys aren't even coming close to hitting us."

"While this is all interesting, I'm beginning to run out of arrows," Abeke said, firing another one in the general direction of their attackers. "So maybe there should be less talk about how we got into this mess, and more discussion about how we're going to escape."

"Perhaps now is a good time to use the Heart of the Land," Anka said. As she pointed a translucent finger toward Rollan, it turned brown to match his cloak. "You still have it, correct?"

Rollan nodded. After returning from the market, he had tied the amulet back around his neck with a leather strap, close to his heart. It fell right where his tattoo of

Essix usually resided—whenever the falcon decided to go into passive state.

Once a large, scaly black rock, the Heart of the Land was now an amber amulet carved into the shape of a gila monster, one of the most feared and famous spirit animals of ancient Amaya. The amulet possessed great powers, but it could also be dangerous if it fell into the wrong hands.

Rollan pulled the stone amulet from under his shirt. "Any thoughts on what power I should use? Maybe I can create a tunnel like last time."

"The tree roots are probably too deep," Abeke said. "Worthy said these trees are hundreds of years old."

"If not older," Conor said. "Maybe you can try an earthquake again?"

"Yeah, I'm thinking that starting an earthquake in the middle of a forest isn't such a good idea," Rollan quipped. "Unless you want tree branches to rain down from the sky."

"I wish we could see where those archers are shooting from," Meilin said. "It's hard to fight an enemy when you can't even see them."

"What about the armor power?" Anka asked. "If we make a run for it, Rollan can take up the rear and block any arrows coming our way."

Rollan shrugged. "Seems like a good idea to me."

Meilin shook her head. Something still didn't feel right about this. But she had delayed them for long enough. "Okay, let's go for it."

"Ready, Briggan?" Conor asked. He slid his ax back into his belt, then scratched the large shaggy wolf on the neck. "Stay close to me."

Meilin noticed Abeke whispering something similar to Uraza. Still uneasy about their decision to retreat, Meilin briefly considered calling forth Jhi. In addition to being a healer, the Great Panda also helped Meilin clear her mind—becoming so calm she could see all sides of a problem, and even slowing down the outside world. Meilin was sure that meditating with Jhi would help illuminate what was troubling her. But they didn't have time for that—and the large, lumbering Jhi and her pristine snow-white fur would be a prime target for the archers.

"We'll go during the next wave," Rollan said. Clutching the Heart of the Land tightly in his right hand, he reached out to Meilin and gave her arm a faint squeeze.

"You should leave your pack behind, Rollan," she said. "You'll move faster without it."

He shook his head. "I'll be fine. Plus, we'll need the supplies later."

"But, Rollan . . ." She stopped as she heard the buzz of arrows in the air. Rollan must have as well. As he scrambled to his feet, the amulet glowed in his hand, his fingers hardly able to contain the amber light leaking through. He thrust his hand in the air as if he was blocking the volley. The arrows froze, hovering for a second, then silently fell to the ground.

Rollan turned and stared at his friends. "What are you waiting for?" he yelled. "Run!"

Conor, Worthy, and Briggan took off, with Abeke close behind. Meilin couldn't see Anka, but she could hear her running ahead, her boots crunching through the forest foliage. She turned to see Rollan behind her, the amulet still glowing in his hands. He paused as another volley approached, then blocked them again.

"Yikes!" Worthy yelled.

Meilin turned to see the Redcloak leaping out of the way of an arrow. It had barely missed him, instead piercing his cloak. Two more arrows sunk into the ground at his feet.

"More archers!" Conor said, pivoting to the left. "Where did they come from?"

Meilin wondered the same thing. From what it seemed, this new set of archers had been sitting in the trees behind them. But if that were the case, they would have had a clear shot at the group. Why hadn't they attacked?

"Keep running!" Rollan yelled, blocking more arrows. But this volley, like so many of the others, hadn't come close to hitting them. Still, the group pivoted again, turning down a small path.

Something about running was helping clear Meilin's mind. These archers were either the worst shots in all of Erdas . . . or they were missing them on purpose! They weren't trying to kill them. They were trying to flush them out. They were funneling them a certain way. . . .

They were running into a trap!

"Guys! We have to stop running! We have to—"

Suddenly, up ahead, Worthy, Conor, and Briggan yelled as a net sprung up from the ground, surrounding them. They flew into the air, crashing into each other as the net spun on the end of a wobbly evergreen tree.

A few feet away, Uraza yowled as another net ensnared her. The leopard tried to find her footing, but there were too many holes in the net for her to gain her balance. The more she struggled, the more tangled she became.

Abeke skidded to a halt. "Don't worry, Uraza! I'll get you out!" She reached for her knife, but then something—Anka, Meilin eventually realized—bumped into Abeke, pushing them both forward. Another net materialized around them, whipping them into the air.

Meilin turned to see Rollan barreling toward her in a full-out sprint. Essix flew above him, her wings spread wide. "Slow down!" Meilin yelled. "It's a—"

But before she could finish her sentence, a tall, wooden cage, sharpened to pinpoint spikes at the top, sprung up around him. Rollan tried to jump over it, but it was too high, even with his spirit animal's help.

"Drop your weapon, Greencloak," a voice said from above. "That is, unless you want a belly full of arrows."

Meilin dropped her quarterstaff as a group of men slithered out of the trees. They were dressed in brown furs, with green and brown paint over their faces. No wonder Meilin hadn't seen them. They were dressed to blend in perfectly with the forest.

She counted them as they exited the trees. There were at least twenty of them, with more still in the forest. One of the men started walking toward them. She recognized him immediately. He was the large, bearded trapper from the trading post, the one that had been doing the most clapping while she danced.

"Check that one first," the man said, pointing to Rollan. "It looked like he was holding something. See what it is."

Rollan held his hands open as two men approached him. They were empty.

"He's clean, Merch," one of the trappers said to the large, bearded man. "Want us to tie him up anyway?"

"Yep." Merch was clearly the one in charge. "And use lots of rope."

"You heard the man," one of the other trappers said, uncoiling a brown rope from around his shoulder. "Stick out your hands."

"Come on, guys," Rollan said, extending his hands through the cage's long vertical bars. "I'm already in a cage. Isn't this a bit overkill." Rollan winced as they tightened their knots. "I think you're cutting off the blood flow to my fingers."

"I'll sure the Oathbound will take you, with or without fingers," Merch replied. "My buddy Cal is already heading back to their camp to let them know that we found you." Picking up a stick, he walked to the net with Conor, Worthy, and Briggan. "And look what we have here," he said, poking at them with the stick. "The mighty Briggan, caught in a net. Guess you aren't such a Great Beast after all."

The wolf snapped at the man. Catching the stick in his strong jaws, Briggan broke off a piece, then hurled it back at him.

"Careful there," Merch taunted. "The Oathbound woman said she wanted the Greencloaks alive. She didn't mention anything about their spirit animals." The man spun the net, stopping it once Worthy was in front of him. "And what exactly are you?" he asked. "Why do your eyes look so funny? And what happened to your hands?"

"Let me out and I'll give you an up-close demonstration," Worthy said, holding up his claws. He tried to reach out and swipe the man, but he was too caught up in the net.

Merch smiled. "Why don't you all put away those precious animals of yours before someone gets hurt?" He poked Briggan again. "Go ahead."

In a flash, Briggan and Uraza disappeared, while Anka slowly came back into view. Although Meilin didn't see Essix, she was sure that the bird was there, hidden out of sight. They were probably going to need her help if they hoped to escape.

"And what about you?" the trapper asked, now pointing his stick at Meilin. "Where's your animal?"

"Already in passive state," Meilin said, showing off Jhi's mark on the back of her hand. "Please don't do this," she continued. "Whatever reward the Oathbound are offering, we'll double it."

He stroked his beard. "Like I could ever trust the word of a Greencloak, especially after the way you all laid waste to Eura." His lips curled into a snarl as he talked.

Rollan shook his hands, vibrating the walls of his cage. "The Oathbound are nothing but big bullies," he said. "We Greencloaks have kept the peace for centuries. If they capture us, they'll split us up and use us as weapons. They'll have each land fighting against one another."

"You have the nerve to talk about Greencloaks keeping the peace?" Merch sneered at Rollan. "Were you keeping the peace a few months ago, when the Greencloaks destroyed my village? When Betarvius fell? Or were you off rampaging some other part of the world?" He neared the cage. "Perhaps you were the one controlling the elk that destroyed the mill. Or maybe it was one of your animals that stampeded through the center of town, destroying all our homes. Or maybe you helped demolish our dam, flooding what little remained of our town." Merch leveled the stick at Rollan. "It was bad enough when the Conquerors came. They stole our animals, seized our supplies. And then, right when we're trying to rebuild, you Greencloaks came along to finish us off. Betarvius was founded by my great-great-grandfather. It stood for hundreds of years. And the Greencloaks destroyed it within a matter of hours."

Meilin glanced at Conor and Worthy. Both their faces were turned to the ground. So that was why they didn't want to talk about Betarvius. It must have fallen after the Greencloaks were taken by the Wyrm. She knew firsthand of the horrors that could be inflicted by a group of people controlled by the Wyrm—she'd seen how the Many had destroyed everything in their path while she was underground in Sadre. There was no village in all of Erdas that could have withstood the might of a horde controlled by the Wyrm, especially if that horde was made up of warriors like the Greencloaks. The village would have been doomed from the start.

Rollan didn't speak for a few moments; he must have understood the gravity of what happened in Betarvius as well. Finally, he said, "I'm sorry about that. Really, I am. But the Greencloaks were under the power of something called the Wyrm—"

"Just more Greencloak lies," Merch said. "We've heard rumors that the queen wants the Greencloaks to disband. We stand with her. It is what's best for Eura."

Rollan opened his mouth again, but Meilin shook her head, warning him to remain quiet. There was nothing Rollan could say that would soothe the man's anger. He had lost too much.

"Since you want to do all this talking, why don't you tell me how you stopped those arrows of ours?" Merch continued. "How did they fall out of the sky like that? It was like they hit an invisible wall or something." Merch jabbed his stick into Rollan's side. A flash of pain came across Rollan's face, but he didn't yell out. The man poked him again, this time harder. "Come on. Spill it."

Finally, Rollan spat out, "I don't know what you're talking about."

"Yeah, you do," he said. "The woman in black told us specifically to watch out for you. Said you had some type of amulet. Some gift."

"You must be imagining things," Rollan said. "Maybe you all just have bad aim."

That drew an even sharper poke from Merch. "Fine, don't tell me. The Oathbound will pry it out of you, one way or another. The way I understand it, the woman leading them, Cordelia the Kind, has a real knack for getting information out of people." He grinned. "She takes the phrase 'kill them with kindness' to a whole new level."

Now Rollan looked worried. "Okay, how about this. If I tell you where it is, will you let us go?"

The man stroked his beard again. "Maybe."

"Don't listen to him, Merch," one of the other trappers said. "You heard what Cordelia said—"

"We'd be long gone by the time she figured it out,"

Merch said. "Think of what we could do with that amulet. We'd be unstoppable. Forget rebuilding Betarvius. We could rule all of Eura!" Merch turned back to Rollan. "So, are you going to tell me or not?"

Rollan opened his mouth, and hesitated.

"Rollan, you can't!" Meilin yelled. He actually looked like he was considering his offer.

"Why not?" Rollan said. "It's better in their hands than the Oathbounds'." Then Rollan smiled and rolled his eyes at her.

It was a signal. Meilin wasn't sure, but she thought it meant that Rollan wanted her to play along.

"Come on, Meilin, what do you say?" Rollan continued. "We give him the amulet, and he lets us go? Just us two. He can still turn the others over to the Oathbound."

"Hey!" Worthy yelled from behind her. She turned to see Conor clamping his hand over the spot on Worthy's mask where his mouth would be. Whatever was happening, Conor wanted it to play out, too.

Meilin took a deep breath. She hoped she was doing what Rollan wanted her to do. "Don't be ridiculous. Look at this guy," she said, nodding toward Merch. "You think he stands a chance against the Oathbound? He could hardly fight his way out of a puddle of water."

Rollan smiled and offered her the slightest of nods. "Meilin, don't fight me on this. It's the only way to save us."

"Us?"

"Yeah. Us," he said. "I'm not leaving without you."

She turned away from him and jutted her chin in the air. "Then I guess we're not leaving."

Rollan sighed. "Merch, buddy, do you mind bringing her over here? Let me talk to her."

Merch cast his eyes upon Meilin, like he was studying her. Like he was trying to figure out if she was really serious.

"Just let me talk to her," Rollan repeated. "Once I get her to change her mind, I'll tell you where the amulet is."

Merch let out a deep grunt, then pointed to two nearby trappers. "Take her over there," he said. "Tie her up to the cage. But watch out for her. She's a fighter. I can see it in her eyes."

Meilin tried to hold her hands apart to keep the rope loose, but this trapper was an expert at knots. He triple-tied the cords, squeezing her hands uncomfortably tight together.

The two trappers then dragged Meilin to the cage. Meilin pulled against them, but they were too strong. They tied her to the side, face-to-face with Rollan.

"Um, how about a little privacy," Rollan said, shooing the men away.

Merch sighed. "Step away, boys. But you two better make it quick."

Rollan shifted forward. They were probably close enough to kiss, although Meilin wasn't trying to think about that.

"If I had known we'd be this close, I would have brushed my teeth," Rollan whispered.

"You can't help yourself, can you? You just can't let the opportunity for a joke to pass you by." Then she smiled. "So what's the plan?"

"Not sure. I'm making this up as I go along."

"Were you at least able to get the amulet to Essix before you were caught?"

"Yeah . . . not quite," he whispered.

"Rollan!" she hissed. "Really?"

"I was hoping to, but Essix was too far away when the cage trapped me. But I was able to slip it into my boot. It's wedged against my ankle. I originally wanted Essix to create a diversion so I could reach it . . ."

"But then you had to mouth off and get yourself tied to the cage."

"Yeah, sorry about that."

"I don't have forever," Merch called out. "You going to tell us where the amulet is or not?"

"Give me another minute," Rollan said. "I've almost got her convinced." Rollan slid even closer to Meilin. "If I was able to get the men away from here, and if Essix created enough of a distraction, do you think you and that big panda of yours can break us out of here?"

"Given our current predicament, I don't see many other options." She shook her head. "But remind me to talk to you about escape strategies."

Rollan smiled, then turned to Merch. "Okay, I'll tell you where it is," he said. "I dropped it in the forest."

Merch threw his stick to the ground. "Boy, is that all you have to say?" Merch pulled a sword from his belt and advanced toward them. It was the falchion, the very sword that Meilin had been drooling over at the trading post. "You tell me where the amulet is, or I start slicing fingers off." He pointed the sword at Meilin. "And I'll start with Twinkle Toes."

"Seriously, it's in the forest," Rollan said "About one hundred paces back. By the oak tree with the large knot in the center. You'll find it if you look hard enough."

Merch glared at both of them. "You'd better not be lying to me. You and your friends' lives depend on it." Merch turned to a small group of nearby men. "You all stay here and keep watch. You others come with me. We need to find that amulet before the Oathbound get here."

Meilin waited until most of the men had disappeared into the forest. Only seven remained, although they were all armed. She looked at Rollan. "Is Essix ready?" she whispered.

"Just give her a signal, and she'll swoop in."

Meilin closed her eyes. In a flash, Jhi appeared beside her. The panda yawned as she took in her surroundings.

"Whoa!" one of the trappers yelled. "Is that a panda?"

"Get it!" another said.

"Don't worry about me," Meilin said to Jhi as the panda began to chew on her rope bonds. "Stop them first."

The panda nodded, turned, and reared up on her hind legs. She roared loud enough to make the birds in the trees take flight. Then she dropped to all fours and charged the men.

The three trappers nearest to them paused for a moment, seemingly frozen by her size, then continued running toward her. They brandished axes and daggers, swinging them wildly in the air as they approached the panda. Meilin knew Jhi could hold her own against the men, but she still worried for her partner. Jhi wasn't the fighting type, though thankfully these men didn't know that.

But just as the men reached Jhi, Essix soared down from a nearby tree. She dove toward the man with a dagger, raking her talons across his face. With streaks of blood across his cheek, he dropped his blade and blindly waved his arms around his head, trying to keep the gyrfalcon away.

"Go, Essix! Get him!" Rollan yelled. "That's what happens when you mess with a Greencloak!"

Meanwhile, Jhi swiped her paws at one of the other trappers, batting him to the ground. She roared again, her bellow loud enough to make the last man drop his weapon and cower before her. But Jhi and Essix didn't have time to waste on those men. Other trappers were already rushing toward the animals. But unlike the first group, these carried crossbows and bolts. Before they could ready their weapons, however, Uraza and Briggan joined the fray, clawing and biting at the men, ripping the crossbows from their hands.

"Hurry up," Rollan said. "I hear the others coming back."

Meilin closed her eyes. She allowed herself to connect to Jhi—to have their thoughts and strengths and souls intertwined. She felt Jhi's strength surge through her. Then she lowered her shoulder, squeezed her eyes shut even tighter, and rammed into the cage. It began to splinter. She rammed it again, this time breaking the wooden bars.

Although her hands were still tied, she could move more freely. She reached through the cage and grabbed Rollan's boot. "Hold on," she said, ripping it from his leg.

"Ouch!" he yelled. "You could be a little gentler, you know."

"Pain—it's an occupational hazard." She turned over the boot, and the Heart of the Land fell to the ground. She picked it up, and tried to hand it to Rollan.

"I can't take it," he said. "My hands are bound too tightly. You use it."

Meilin looked at the small stone. She curled her fingers around the amulet, then thrust it into the sky. It began to give off its bright amber glow.

"Um, Meilin," Rollan began. "What exactly are you about to do?"

"What do you think?"

"Remember what we were talking about a little while ago," he said, his words faster. "About how earthquakes weren't so good when surrounded by huge trees and thick branches and—"

"Brace yourself!" she yelled. She struck her hand hard against the ground.

Thunder boomed, and a shock wave radiated from Meilin on out. The trappers bobbed, trying to keep their balance as the earth rolled underneath them. All around them, branches and tree trunks creaked and snapped upon being hit by vibration after vibration.

Meilin leaped out of the way right before a tree limb crashed to the ground, barely missing her. Likewise, the branches holding the others came crashing down.

"Ouch," Conor yelled.

"Oomp," said Worthy.

"Sorry," Meilin muttered. She took in the scene. While the trappers wobbled to their feet, Abeke and Conor began cutting through their thick ropes. But they were slow, and the trappers were already lurching forward.

"Hit them again!" Rollan yelled, bracing himself against the cage.

Meilin struck her fist back into the ground. More trees fell, and the trappers once again stumbled off their feet. Abeke grabbed Anka and rolled to her left as a huge tree limb came thundering down. Across from them, Worthy and Conor had worked their way out of their net, and were now getting to their feet.

Worthy ran toward a group of men. "You guys like to shoot arrows from afar. Let's see how you do up close." He leaped at the men, landing on one of their backs and flipping him over. "I'll take care of these men," Worthy said. "Free Abeke and Anka!"

Conor nodded, then rushed to help the others. Meilin started to run toward them as well, but stopped as she heard footsteps approaching.

"Meilin, behind you!" Rollan yelled.

She turned to see the rest of the hunters rushing toward her. Merch was in the front, waving his sword high in the air.

"Jhi, help me!" Meilin called out as she charged the men. Feeling Jhi's power coursing through her body once again, she leaped into the air and landed a round-house kick squarely on one of the trapper's jaws. Then she spun around, kicking two more to the ground.

Essix appeared beside her, taking out another trapper before he could fire his arrow at her. Then there was Jhi, back on her hind paws, swatting down the men as soon as they drew near. Her coat was wet with blood—Meilin hoped that it belonged to one of the attackers, not the panda.

"Yikes," Rollan yelled. "A little help here?"

Meilin turned to see Merch and two trappers running toward Rollan. The boy, still tied to the cage, was defenseless.

Meilin took off, channeling Jhi's massive power into her legs. Using a fallen tree, she catapulted herself over the men, landing between them and Rollan.

Merch seemed surprised for a moment, then his mouth curled into a snarl. "Doesn't seem fair, does it?" Merch said, waving the sword at her. "Us with the weapons and you with nothing but your hands tied together."

"Yeah, it's not fair. For you!" Jumping into the air, she kneed the first trapper in the nose, then kicked him in the chest, hurling him backward. She flipped back to her feet and charged toward the second man. But before she could reach him, an arrow whizzed past Meilin and sunk into his shoulder. A second later Uraza was at the man's side, clamping her sharp teeth into his leg.

Meilin turned quickly to thank Abeke, then focused on Merch. "That's a nice sword," she said. "Do you mind if I take it?"

"Sure, you can have it as soon as I run you through with it." Merch lurched forward, and Meilin expertly dodged his thrust. Meilin grabbed his arm, spun around, and flipped him over her shoulder.

When he opened his eyes, he was lying upside down against what remained of the wooden cage. And Meilin was holding the falchion between her still-tied hands.

"What were you saying about this sword?" she asked, a large smile on her face.

Around her, most of the other trappers had either given up or had fled into the forest. She waved at Jhi as the Great Panda sat on top of one of the trappers, stopping him from trying to escape.

"Now that's the kind of fighting I like," Rollan said. "The type where I don't have to lift a finger." He jutted his hands toward Meilin. "But if you don't mind, I would really appreciate it if you got me out of here."

She opened her hand, revealing the Heart of the Land. "Want me to use the earthquake powers one last—"

"No!" Rollan, Conor, and Abeke yelled at the same time.

She laughed. "Come on, guys. Can't you take a joke?"

Rollan rolled his eyes as Conor began to cut him free. "You stick to fighting. I'll handle the jokes."

TRUNSWICK

AFTER TALKING IT OVER, THEY DECIDED TO TIE UP the remaining trappers. Conor didn't like this idea–really, no one did–but they didn't have any other options. Using the wood and nets from their own traps, Conor and the others created a large cage to hold them all. The men were cramped, but it would keep them safe from any dangerous beasts wandering through the forest. Based on what the trappers had told them, it would take their companion, Cal, a full day to reach the Oathbound campsite. Adding another day for the return trip, and Conor figured that they only had a two-day head start. It would be risky, but they decided to travel during the daytime–which meant traveling with their spirit animals in passive state. Conor knew Briggan enjoyed roaming the countryside, but they had to make it to Trunswick before the Oathbound found them.

Just before they were about to leave, Conor walked over to Merch, the leader of the trappers.

"You can't leave us out here like this," Merch said. "We'll starve."

"We left you plenty of food and water," Conor said. "Your friend will be back soon."

"But what if he's delayed? What if he's lost?"

"Don't worry. Someone will come for you." Conor knelt in front of the man. "Also, I just wanted to say, I'm sorry for your loss," he added quietly. "How many people survived?"

Merch's eyes softened, if only for an instant. "Just the handful of us trappers who were out in the forest." Then just as quickly, his gaze turned cold. "Tell me the truth. Were you there?"

"I was not there," Conor said. But he may as well have been. He, like all the other infected people, had done terrible things. Sure, he could argue that it wasn't his fault, but that didn't undo the pain he and the other Greencloaks had inflicted on innocent people.

"I know you don't trust us," Conor said. "But I promise, the Greencloaks will make this right. We won't rest until we've helped rebuild all of Erdas, including Betarvius."

"I've seen your help," Merch said. He spat onto the ground, then wiped his mouth with the back of his hand. "I'll take my chances with the Oathbound."

"Merch, just listen to me—"

"Conor," Abeke said. Like usual, he hadn't heard her approach. "We need to go." She placed her hand gently on his shoulder. "Come."

"I'm sorry," Conor said one last time as Merch turned away from him. He stood and picked up his ax. It felt much too heavy in his hands.

"Conor, I know you feel sorry for these men, but we have to keep focused on our mission," Abeke said as they went to join the others.

"Yeah," Conor said. "It's just that, ever since I was a little kid, I've always wanted people to like me. I hated disappointing anyone—even Worthy, when I was his servant. I wish there was something I could say to Merch to make him feel better."

"Hopefully his heart will soften. But it will take time. Years, perhaps. But just because his heart is made of stone doesn't mean yours needs to carry the same weight."

"Thanks, Abeke. You really are a true friend."

"And I'll *always* be your friend," she said. "Now come. We have to move quickly."

They started off toward Trunswick, now taking the main roads. They knew they'd encounter more people, but it would cut their travel time by a full day. At night, they stopped long enough for a few hours of sleep, then kept moving, using the moon to illuminate their way. Instead of cooking their meals, they ate cold roots and plants that they dug up along the roadside.

Conor's heart swelled the closer they got to town. He found himself marveling at childhood landmarks— the creek his father tossed him into when he was first learning to swim. The hill he often took his sheep to for grazing. The fence he mended for the Widow Tomball for a few coins—which he promptly returned to her after feeling guilty for taking her money.

Worthy wouldn't admit it, but he was clearly growing nervous about returning home. Instead of becoming excited and speeding their journey homeward along, Worthy kept slowing down. He complained about entering the town at night—said he didn't want to get into a skirmish with the gate sentries. Then he protested about their dinner of wild mushrooms, demanding that they stop and cook a proper meal.

Finally, after he stalled the group because he thought he'd sprained his ankle on a tree root, Conor pulled Worthy to the side, trailing behind the others. "What's wrong? Aren't you excited to go home?"

"Of course I am," Worthy hissed back. "But as soon as we reach Trunswick, they'll find out that I don't exactly know where the records are."

Conor snapped his fingers. He'd forgotten about his conversation with Worthy on the ship. "You have to tell them," Conor said. "Now. And if you don't, I will."

"But they'll hate me," Worthy said.

"Trust me, they'll dislike you even more the longer you deceive them."

"I'll tell them. I promise. As soon as we're safely inside the city." Worthy pressed his hands together and fell to his knees. "Please, Conor. Let me just have a little bit longer."

Conor stared at Worthy, then slowly shook his head. He really was too nice sometimes. "Fine," he said. "But you have to tell them as soon as we reach the manor."

"Deal!" Worthy said. He sprung to his feet, and they joined up with the others.

"What should we expect when we're there?" Meilin asked. "Did the Greencloaks attack your town as well?"

Conor shook his head. "According to my parents, the fighting stopped just south of Trunswick. That's when Zerif called all the Greencloaks back for the final battle."

"Anything else we need to know about Trunswick?" Rollan asked. "After my last slipup about towns in the area, I want to be prepared."

Worthy shrugged. "Um, no . . . I don't think there's anything else you need to know. Everything's just fine. Nothing strange happened. Nothing burned down or anything like that."

"Huh?" Anka asked. "Worthy, what are you talking about?"

"He's just nervous about seeing his brother," Conor said, stepping in for Worthy. "He's always a bit of a mess when he's excited."

Rollan snorted. "Then he must *always* be excited." He turned to Conor. "Are you going to take us in by the secret back entrance? It's pretty close to the castle, right?" Conor hadn't realized that Rollan had remembered that. They'd traveled to Trunswick while on a mission to find Rumfuss the Boar; it had been Conor's first time back in the town since becoming a Greencloak. He'd wanted to impress Rollan, but had ended up being embarrassed in front of him, thanks to Devin and his father. Then, to make matters worse, the Earl of Trunswick threw them in jail.

He hoped this visit ended on a better note.

"Worthy may have a better way for us to enter," Conor eventually said. "He knows the town better than I do. He'll take the lead once we're there."

Worthy jumped in the air, waving his fists. "Don't worry, guys. You can depend on me!"

Meilin pointed her new sword at Worthy's feet. "I thought you sprained your ankle," she said. "Did it magically heal up?"

"Oops," Worthy said as he immediately began limping again. "It comes and goes. Joints are tricky like that."

Rollan shook his head. "Worthy, you're favoring the wrong foot."

It was well past midnight when they first caught sight of the town. Trunswick sat on a large hill, its sandy-colored walls reaching high to the sky.

"That's funny," Rollan said. "I would have thought that we'd be able to see the castle from here."

"Ah, it must be too cloudy," Worthy mumbled.

Conor winced as Rollan looked up. A bright moon hung overhead. There wasn't a cloud in sight.

"Now follow me," Worthy continued, stepping off the path. "I know another way past the town gates."

Worthy led them through an abandoned field until they reached a small drainage pipe at the base of the wall. After a few tugs, he and Conor were able to pry the small iron gate from the pipe opening. They crept into the city, single file. A few torchlights illuminated the streets, but otherwise the town was silent.

"No guards?" Rollan asked. "That's unusual."

Conor had to agree. Usually, there was always a sentry or guard roaming the streets or keeping watch at one of the walled towers. But now, everything seemed silent.

"We lost a lot of our guards right after the war," Worthy said. "Father wasn't always the best at paying people fairly."

They turned a corner, then froze, staring speechlessly at the shell of a building standing before them. Finally, Meilin said, "Um, Worthy, what happened to your castle?"

Trunswick Manor—once five stories high with massive sandstone towers that pierced the sky—was now a lump of charred bricks, crumbling walls, and splintered wood. One tower remained, half burned and leaning heavily against the manor's interior walls. A tattered, soot-coated blue flag flew from the tower, one of the only reminders that this had once been the mighty structure. Miraculously, the giant double-doored entrance and archway remained standing, though the walls surrounding it had long fallen. The manor grounds, once immaculate, were now overrun with vines and thorny bushes.

Worthy let out a long, deep breath. "There was a little accident."

"That doesn't look little," Meilin said.

"So where exactly are we going?" Anka asked. "Worthy, if you're just leading us on some wild-goose chase—"

"I'm not! I promise." He started off toward the outskirts of the walled town. "Follow me. We'll be at Dawson's, um, *estate* soon."

Worthy led them through the town's empty dirt streets, eventually stopping at a small wooden cottage.

"This is the new Trunswick Manor?" Conor asked. He knew that Dawson was no longer living in the castle, but he hadn't expected him to be living in a *cottage*. It wasn't much bigger than his family's home out in the countryside.

Worthy softly knocked on the door using a long, intricate rhythm. When no one answered, he repeated the knock.

Conor could see what looked like a candle illuminating the window beside the door. "Who is it?" someone from inside called.

"Tellun the Elk," Worthy said. "Who else do you think would use our secret knock?"

The door flung open. Dawson stood in a long wool nightgown, holding a candle. Rumfuss the Boar stood beside him, his tusks white and pointed.

"Devin!" Dawson placed the candle on an end table, then leaped forward, embracing his brother in a long hug. "I can't believe you're here!" He pulled back to get a good look at Worthy, then hugged him again.

Unlike everyone else that they had encountered, Dawson didn't seem frightened or shocked by his brother's new look. He loved his brother, no matter what.

"I'm all for family reunions," Rollan said. "But can we take this inside? We do have a bounty out for our heads, after all."

"Yes, of course," Dawson said, leading them in. Once inside, he double-bolted the door. Conor and Abeke released their spirit animals. Briggan and Uraza immediately went to Rumfuss, sniffing him and nudging him with their noses. Meilin then released Jhi, but instead of walking toward the others, she sat down and began to eat Dawson's spruce plant.

"Sorry about that," Meilin said. "It's been a while since she's eaten."

Dawson shrugged. "No problem. It was my father's

plant anyway." He turned as something moved behind him. "There's another old friend here that wants to say hello."

A small black cat leaped onto a low bookshelf behind Dawson.

"Kunaya!" Abeke said. The cat sprinted nimbly along the edge of the shelf then jumped into Abeke's outstretched arms. Uraza looked at the cat and let off a low growl.

"Don't be jealous," Abeke said as she stroked the cat. "Kunaya's an old friend of ours."

Worthy walked over to take a peek at the cat, when she suddenly meowed and jumped into his arms. "It looks like you two have a history as well," Abeke said.

"A little," Worthy said. Cradling the cat, he sat down in one of the few chairs in the room. "I like what you've done with the place, Dawson." He nodded toward a blue tapestry hanging on the wall. "You were able to save the family crest."

"It was about the only thing that didn't burn down," Dawson said. "Though it took me three hours to scrub all the soot and smoke out of the fabric."

"Speaking of that," Meilin began. "Maybe now would be a good time to explain what's been happening around here." She cut her eyes to Worthy. "Apparently, someone's been keeping a few secrets from us."

"So, where to begin . . ." Dawson said. "As I'm sure you realized, Trunswick Castle is gone. Devin burned it down the last time he was here."

"It wasn't my fault." He paused as he placed the black cat on the floor. "Well, it wasn't *completely* my fault. I was having a bad day."

"This was after he started a riot, of course," Dawson said.

Worthy hesitated. "Okay, that one really was all my fault. But I did it for a good reason."

Meilin leaned forward. "Why didn't you tell us any of this?"

He shrugged. "I wanted you to like me. And I didn't keep it from everyone," he said. "I told Conor."

Conor's friends all leveled their gazes on him. "Thanks, Worthy," Conor mumbled. It was just like Worthy to pull Conor into his web of lies. "I'm sorry, guys. I probably should have made Worthy tell you all. But I still think coming to Trunswick was the right call."

"Perhaps," Meilin said. "But you should have trusted us to make that decision together. With *all* the information."

Conor wished he could disappear. He was no longer a servant to the Trunswicks, but he was still getting into trouble because of them.

"We have to remember, we're all fighting for the same thing," Abeke said. "So from now on, no more secrets. Agreed? Unified until the end."

They all nodded. Conor expected Rollan to crack a joke or two, but he remained silent, instead rubbing his brown cloak between his fingers.

"Dawson, were you able to save anything else from the castle?" Worthy asked. "Down in the lower levels, there were some records on old parchment. I looked through them once, when father was away. I thought I saw something about a powerful sword there. The Wildcat's Claw. Our family sword was modeled after it."

"A lot of those records were damaged by the water used to put out the fire," Dawson said. "We took everything we could salvage and moved it to the Howling House. That's probably where you should start."

"The Howling House!" Rollan yelled. "I have to go back to *that* place?"

"What's the Howling House?" Anka asked. Conor looked around until he noticed the blurry shape leaning against the door.

"It's a prison where they keep innocent people," Rollan said. "Cat-boy over there threw me and Conor into it the first time I visited this place."

"Sorry about that," Worthy said. "To be fair, I really did hate Greencloaks at the time. You guys were just so . . . *smug*. It wasn't fair."

"The Howling House *was* where we kept people affected by bonding sickness," Dawson said. "But we don't use it that way anymore. We have no need for it, since there's no more bonding sickness. Plus, we don't exactly have the funds for its upkeep." He turned to his brother. "Have you heard about father?"

The air seemed to escape from the room. "What's wrong?" Worthy asked quietly. "Is he . . . dead?"

Dawson shook his head. "No, but after you hear this, you might wish he was. He abandoned the town—and our family—taking every coin, gem, and valuable he could find with him. The town is broke, but we *are* rebuilding . . . slowly. Our military is gone, now replaced by a militia made up of farmers and other townsfolk. Mother and Daphne have decided not to return, and with you off helping the Redcloaks, the citizens chose *me* as the new Earl of Trunswick."

Dawson sighed, looking older and wearier than Conor had ever believed he could. "At this point I'm mostly a figurehead, but I'll do everything in my power to help our people."

Dawson had always been the kindest member of his family. He had treated Conor with respect, even when Conor was just a lowly servant boy. Dawson was young, but of all the Trunswicks, he was the right person to lead the town.

"Why you?" Worthy asked. "With the way father disgraced our family and fled the town, why would they pick *any* Trunswick to serve as earl? I mean, I'm sure you'll do the best you can, but you don't know the first thing about running a city. You're just a kid."

Dawson stood taller as he crossed his arms. "You're a kid, too. You all are. But that doesn't stop you from doing your duty, does it?" He relaxed a little as Rumfuss hoofed over to him. "And to be honest, I think it has more to do with Rumfuss than my amazing leadership skills. His name carries way more weight than ours right now."

Beside Dawson, the Great Boar snuffled proudly.

"But there's one other problem," Dawson said, sinking into the other chair in the room. "You're all wanted criminals. According to the rumors, you assassinated the Emperor of Zhong."

"We didn't kill him," Conor said. "He was murdered by people pretending to be Greencloaks."

"I'm sure I don't have to tell you what the public perception of Greencloaks is right now." Dawson's gaze became sharp. In a moment, he looked as shrewd as his father. "There's word that the queen wants to dismantle your order. She says the Marked would be of better use in service to their respective lands."

"And what do you think?" Conor asked.

Dawson leaned over and patted Rumfuss on the back. The boar grunted, then rolled over on his back so the boy could reach his stomach. "I've seen firsthand what the Wyrm did. I also saw how you Greencloaks fought against it. I stand with you. You have my full support."

Worthy pulled his cloak around him. "Don't forget, me and the Redcloaks were there, too."

Dawson laughed. "Of course. The Wyrm wouldn't have been defeated without the Redcloaks."

Worthy sat up in his chair. "Do the townsfolk know that I'm a Redcloak?" There was an air of hope in his voice. "Do they know what I did to help save the world?"

Dawson rubbed the back of his head as he sighed. "Devin, I'll always see you as a hero. But I can't speak for the rest of the town. You were cruel to a lot of people. You became even more of a bully when you obtained that fake spirit animal. And then, when you finally returned home with your tail between your legs—no pun intended—you started a riot right in the middle of the square."

"I had a good reason," Worthy said. "I was trying to save a defenseless woman."

Abeke had picked up Kunaya and was now stroking the cat again. "You don't have to lie to us anymore, Worthy," she said. "You've proven yourself. You don't have to boast about your deeds."

"Yeah," Rollan said. "Everyone makes mistakes. Even me, every once in a while."

"I'm not lying!" Worthy yelled. "I really was trying to save a woman! She was in the stocks in the square." He turned to his brother. "Tell them, Dawson."

His brother shrugged. "The way I heard it, the people began to riot because you were boasting about father's wealth."

"No, it wasn't like that," Worthy said. "I mean, yes, it was, but I was saying all that on purpose. I was trying to free the woman—"

"As interesting as this sounds, we should probably head to the Howling House," Meilin said. "We've already wasted enough time."

"It's too late to go now," Dawson said. "The sun will be rising in less than an hour. The militia will start their first patrol soon." He rose and opened the closer of two doors. A cramped bedroom waited within. "You all can stay here for now. It'll be a tight fit, but it should serve you well enough. Tomorrow night, you can sneak to the Howling House to find what you need."

Conor looked out of the window. The darkness was fading away. In another hour, his parents would be awake, tending to their animals.

"Hey, Worthy, can I talk to you for a second?" Rollan asked, walking toward the bedroom. He was carrying his large pack. "I want to get your, um, opinion on something really quick."

Meilin and Abeke looked at each other as the two boys disappeared into the room. "I don't even want to know what that's about," Meilin said.

Conor crossed the room then knelt beside Dawson. Rumfuss huffed as Conor entered their space. "Do you think it's safe enough for me to visit my family?" Conor asked.

Dawson shook his head. "Sorry, Conor. That would be too risky. But I just saw them last week. They're doing well. Your brothers are good shepherds." Dawson tilted his head. "You favor your oldest brother quite a bit. His face is a little rounder, though." Dawson looked at the ground for a moment, then back up. "I try to look out for your family as much as I can. It's the least I can do." He suddenly grabbed Conor's hand. "Conor, can you ever forgive me for deceiving you like that?"

Conor frowned. "What are you talking about?"

"The letter," he said softly. "Remember the letter about your mother? And the Iron Boar?"

As soon as Dawson mentioned the Iron Boar, Conor knew exactly what he meant. Conor and his friends had successfully located Rumfuss's Iron Boar talisman, a mystic item that granted the wearer an almost impenetrable armor-like skin. It was a power similar to the gila monster's amulet, Conor thought. But then the Earl of Trunswick threatened Conor's mother, forcing him to turn over the Iron Boar for her safety. Dawson had been the one to deliver his father's demands.

Conor had never been more ashamed of himself as he turned over the talisman for his mother's safety. He'd betrayed his friends, and the green cloak he was so proud to wear.

"There isn't a day that's passed where I didn't wish I could go back and change things," Dawson said.

"I should have tried to help you. I should have pushed back against my father."

"We've both made mistakes," Conor said. "But now's our chance for us to redeem ourselves."

Dawson seemed comforted by this. Surprisingly, so was Conor.

RACE AGAINST
THE MILITIA

ABEKE AND THE OTHERS SPENT MOST OF THE DAY trying to rest. Conor, Worthy, and Rollan had bunked in the room with Dawson, leaving Abeke, Meilin, and Anka to share the other small room. They had allowed Anka to take the bed and had used Dawson's extra quilts to cushion the wooden floor. It wasn't the most comfortable of sleeping arrangements, but it was much better than the cold, unforgiving ground along Eura's country roads.

The sun had set an hour ago. Now they were just waiting for the last of the shops to close in the market. They wanted the streets as empty as possible before they started the trek to the Howling House.

Abeke counted and organized the arrows in her remaining quiver while Meilin finished her training lesson with Anka. They had been working on punching techniques. Meilin was trying to get Anka to step forward while delivering her punch, as a way to maximize her power. Anka kept doing the opposite, however, punching while rocking backward on her heels. As they trained, Abeke realized this was one of the few times she'd had a chance to study Anka—she was always so hard to see with her chameleon powers. She wasn't the best warrior by a long shot, but Meilin seemed determined to train her. However, what Anka lacked in fighting skills she more than made up for with stealth. Even with the help of Uraza's heightened senses, it often took Abeke a few moments to locate Anka when she was invisible.

There was a soft knock on the door, and a moment later, Rollan pushed it open. "You all should come out and hear this for yourselves," he said. "It's important."

Anka and Meilin bowed toward each other, finishing their sparring. In a flash, Anka's chameleon appeared on her shoulder. The green animal blinked his wide, bulging eyes a few times as he took in his surroundings. Then, as he scampered along Anka's collarbone, the animal slowly faded to green and brown, matching the wall behind them. A few seconds later, Anka faded away into a similar wavy haze.

They entered the main room to see Dawson and the others standing around the table. A brown parchment stretched out across the tabletop.

"We've got trouble," Dawson said. "According to some of the shopkeepers, soldiers in black uniforms were in the city, looking for five renegade Greencloaks and a mysterious warrior in red."

"The Oathbound caught up with us sooner than I thought," Worthy said. He read the parchment again and stroked his chin. "At least they called me a warrior."

"The woman in charge was offering a hefty reward," Dawson continued. "Enough to feed some families for half a year, if not longer."

"Did they leave?" Meilin asked.

"About an hour ago," Dawson said. "They were heading west, along the river. But I'd bet all the bristles on Rumfuss's back that they'll return tomorrow. Probably with more soldiers." Rumfuss burrowed between Dawson's legs and settled underneath the table. "Understandably, the captain of the militia is worried. She's requested more militiamen to patrol the streets tonight. I could try to talk her out of it, but that would cause more suspicion."

Abeke ran her finger along the edge of her bow. "So either we remain in hiding for a few days until things calm down, or we take our chances and go now."

"I think we should go," Meilin said. "We can't afford to wait. The risk for failure is too great."

The others nodded in agreement.

"It'll be difficult to hide all six of us," Anka said. "Especially if we're moving."

"Then we should split up," Abeke said. "Anka will hide as many as she can, and the rest of us will follow."

"But what about all that talk about being united?" Worthy asked.

"United in our duty to one another and to the Greencloaks." Abeke paused as she noticed Worthy's arms were crossed peevishly. "I mean, Greencloaks *and* Redcloaks." Seeing him relax, she continued. "United in our mission . . . but not necessarily in *how* we execute that mission."

"Conor and Worthy, you should go with Anka," Meilin said. "We can't risk anyone recognizing you."

Conor rolled up his sleeve and stretched out his bare arm. "Come on, Briggan. Best go into passive." The wolf glanced at Conor and gave a soft whimper. "Oh, don't look at me like that. I'll let you back out as soon as we get to the Howling House." The wolf stood up, shaking fur across everyone. The room flashed, and Briggan disappeared onto Conor's arm.

Uraza paused from cleaning her paws with her tongue to look at Abeke. She blinked her purple eyes at her inquisitively. "Don't worry; you don't have to go into passive state. At least, not yet," Abeke said.

Conor slipped on the coat he'd borrowed from Dawson. It was a little snug, but would have to do. "Rollan, you'd better come with us, too, just to be on the safe side. People may remember you from the last time that you were here with me."

Rollan's shoulders sagged, but he nodded. Everyone knew he'd rather travel with Meilin. He picked up his brown cloak—now covered with Briggan's excess fur— and fastened it around his neck. "You don't ever hear anyone complaining about a falcon shedding," he mumbled.

"We'll meet you as soon as we can," Meilin said. She picked up her quarterstaff and offered it to Anka. "You should carry a weapon. Just remember our training and you'll be fine."

"Thank you." As Anka took it, the wooden staff turned invisible. "You guys ready?" she asked.

Rollan, Conor, and Worthy nodded. A few seconds later, they disappeared before Abeke's eyes.

"Whoa!" Dawson looked at Rumfuss. "We've got to get some cool tricks like that."

"You'll discover even more powers, in time," Abeke said. "If you joined the Greencloaks, we could help you with your training."

Dawson hesitated, then said, "Thank you for the offer, but my place is here in Trunswick."

"Yeah, and if he joins anything, it'll be the Redcloaks!" Worthy said.

"Okay, enough talking," Anka said. The door slowly opened. "See you soon."

They listened as four sets of footsteps exited the house. Then the door closed shut.

Dawson stood in the middle of the room shaking his head. "How do you guys get used to that? That was awesome."

"Believe me, we've seen stranger." Meilin slid the falchion out of its scabbard and inspected the blade. "What's the best way to get to the Howling House?"

"The most direct way is straight through town. It's right past the castle. Or what's left of the castle." Dawson opened the door again and peeked out. "Okay, the coast is clear. You can go."

"We should take the rooftops," Meilin said. "It'll be easier to avoid the militia."

Abeke and Meilin quickly slipped out of the cottage and stepped into an empty alleyway. Meilin looked up and measured the distance. "I could make it up there on my own, but a little help never hurt." Moments later,

Jhi appeared by Meilin's side. She nuzzled the animal's snout. "How about it, Jhi? Care to give me a little power boost?"

Both Meilin and Jhi closed their eyes, almost as if they were in a trance. Seconds later, Meilin exploded into a run. She leaped against the wall of the first building, letting her foot hit the side of the fading brick, then pivoted and launched herself toward the other building. She went like this back and forth until she reached the top.

She leaned over the edge, then curtsied for Abeke.

Abeke walked over to the Great Panda as she sat there, looking up at Meilin. "Are you jumping up there as well, Jhi?"

Meilin laughed as she stretched out her arms. "She would much rather take the easy way up," she said, calling back Jhi.

Abeke let her fingers run along the back of Uraza's lush fur. "Come on, Uraza. We can do better than that, right?" And then, as the leopard's power coursed between them, they took off up the wall.

Abeke loved running across the rooftops with Uraza on her heels. It wasn't the plains of the savannah outside of her village in Nilo, but she was still having a blast. The wind stirred around them, making it almost feel like they were in an empty field instead of a walled city. After so much fighting and seriousness, it was good to just let loose and run.

Even without her spirit animal aiding her, Meilin was

doing an excellent job of keeping up. The girl even did a couple of flips as she jumped across some alleyways—probably just to show off, like Worthy had done in the forest. Abeke hadn't minded then, and she didn't mind now. After so much fighting, they could all use a little fun.

Eventually, Abeke and Meilin traveled as far as they could above the city. In the distance, past the charred, crumbling remains of Trunswick Castle, stood the Howling House.

"We won't have any cover until we get to the castle," Abeke said.

Meilin nodded as she surveyed the area around them. "I don't see any militia. I think we should chance it."

They shinnied down the side of the building, then took off across the open street. They had almost reached the castle grounds when Abeke heard footsteps behind them.

"Hey! Stop there!" a man yelled. He held a lantern in one hand and a sword in the other. Two other men chased behind him. Their blue tunics matched the colors of the city crest.

"Almost made it," Meilin said. "Now what?"

"Maybe we could lose him in the castle," Abeke offered.

The girls sprinted across the overgrown lawn, leaping over blackened stone boulders and charred wood. They scurried over a fallen column, past the stone archway, and raced inside the castle walls. A long, winding staircase stood before them. The staircase looked like it was made of brass, but there was too much ash coating it to know for sure.

"That way," Meilin said, rushing up the stairs to what remained of the second floor. "They'd be fools to follow us up here."

The steps creaked and groaned underneath them as they neared the top landing. Abeke was sure they would buckle any second. "Um, now who exactly are the fools again?" Abeke asked. Taking the last three steps in one bound, she landed heavily on the second floor, which sagged beneath her. Uraza landed beside her, stirring up a cloud of ash. "Maybe this wasn't such a good idea."

"If it was a bad idea for us, then it's a horrible idea for them," Meilin said, pointing to the militiamen following them up the stairs. "Do you see how they're handling their weapons? They aren't soldiers. They should be holding shepherds crooks, not swords."

"My village doesn't have any dedicated soldiers, either," Abeke said as they took cover behind an overturned bust of a man. Abeke couldn't be sure, but she assumed that it was a statue of Dawson and Worthy's father. "If and when the time comes for battle, all able-bodied men are expected to fight, whether they're teachers or hunters."

"Even if they aren't trained?" Meilin asked.

She nodded. "Of course, it was always frowned upon if a woman ever wanted to—" Abeke stopped as a light shone above them.

"Hey, I see you!" one of the men yelled. "Stop. You're trespassing."

"Save that thought," Meilin said, taking off down the grand hallway. "Come on!"

Abeke took off after her, turning as the hallway split and intersected with other smaller hallways.

Abeke slowed as she sidestepped a cracked chandelier. Shards of glass had exploded across the entire swath of carpet. The glass fragments shone from the moonlight pouring through the collapsed ceiling. "Watch your step," Abeke warned Uraza. "You don't want to get glass in between your paws."

Meilin screeched to a halt, almost causing Abeke to run into her. The entire hallway floor in front of them was cracked and splintered, with large holes gaping through the floorboards. Below, Abeke saw what looked like a grand parlor.

"There's no way that floor will hold us, especially running at full speed." Meilin called forth Jhi. "But I bet we can jump it."

Nodding, Abeke backed up a few paces. Then, just as the militiamen turned into the hallway, Meilin, Abeke, and Uraza raced and leaped across the aging wood, easily clearing it.

The men stood, their weapons hanging at their sides, as Jhi disappeared.

"You're the Greencloaks the Oathbound are looking for!" one man yelled. He accusingly thrust his sword toward them. "Stop! Turn yourselves in!"

Meilin shook her head. "Not going to happen."

"You don't know the entire truth," Abeke said. "The Oathbound are not what they seem!"

"They said you killed the Emperor of Zhong and that you tried to kill the Queen of Eura."

"Lies!" Abeke said.

"We're not going to change their minds, and we're running out of time," Meilin said. "Just shoot them and let's get this over with."

Abeke gasped. "Meilin!"

Meilin shrugged. "What? I didn't say kill them. Just shoot them in the shoulder or leg or something so they'll stop chasing us."

"By order of the Queen of Eura, we hereby place you under arrest," one of the other militiamen yelled, his voice quavering. He looked young, barely older than them. He held a rapier in his shaking hand.

Meilin sighed as she unsheathed her sword. "Guys, seriously. Do you not see that she has a leopard? And I have a giant panda. And you all . . . you can barely hold your weapons."

"Meilin, you're not helping," Abeke whispered.

"Trust me," Meilin whispered back. Then, looking back at the men, she said, "Come on! Or are you too scared to fight two girls?"

The men held their weapons higher. "For Trunswick!" the leader roared. "Charge!"

"No!" Abeke yelled. "Wait!"

But it was too late. As soon as the men surged forward, the floor underneath them opened up. As the floorboards cracked, the men fell to the lower story.

Meilin sheathed her sword and dusted off her hands. "Well, that's done. Let's go."

"We can't just leave them," Abeke said.

"We don't have time—"

"They were just doing their duty," Abeke said. She listened for a few seconds. Thanks to Uraza, she could make out three district groans. "At least they're still alive."

Meilin sighed. "All right, fine. Let's help them." They slowly walked to the edge of the large hole and peered down. The men lay in a heap on the floor. "Do you yield?" Meilin asked.

"Never," one of the men said. Then he passed out.

Abeke and Meilin leaped to the bottom floor. Abeke drew her bow and aimed an arrow at them, although she quickly realized this was pointless. The men were in no condition to fight.

Returning her arrow to the quiver, Abeke collected the men's weapons. "I'm sorry for the pain we caused you," she said. "We mean you no harm."

Meilin knelt in front of the youngest of the men as he cradled his arm. "Don't move," she said. He winced as she touched his wrist. "I don't think it's broken. Merely sprained. Hold on for a second."

She called forth Jhi, and the man shrank away. "Don't hurt me!" he yelled.

"We're not going to attack you," Meilin said. "Jhi is a healer. She'll help." The large panda lumbered to the man, then began licking his hand and arm. Slowly, he slumped to the ground and sighed in relief.

"These two seem fine," Abeke said. The other man had regained consciousness. She helped both of them to their feet. "Are you hurt? Any broken bones? Jhi can help you, too."

"Nothing hurt but my pride," the leader said. "You're really not going to kill us?"

"Of course not," Abeke said. "But we *will* have to tie you up for a while," she added sheepishly. "But don't worry—we'll send someone back for you."

The leader of the men shook his head. "But the Oathbound . . . they said you were murderers. They said you would destroy us all."

"We're Greencloaks," Meilin said. "We are protectors. The Oathbound are the dangerous ones."

The leader looked at the other man, then nodded. "Their leader, Cordelia the Kind, said she'd destroy the town if she discovered you were here," he said. "I'm sorry. We were just trying to protect ourselves."

"We know," Meilin said. "You three were very brave. You can tell your friends all about your adventures and embellish as much as you want . . . tomorrow." She placed her hand on her sword. "But for right now, we're going to need to tie you up. And quickly. We have someplace to be."

THE MIGHTY WILCO

ROLLAN'S MUSCLES INVOLUNTARILY FLEXED AS HE heard footsteps creaking above them. He wasn't sure if the others heard it–they were farther back in the basement, away from the stairs. Pausing from reading the large journal in front of him, he grabbed a torch from the wall sconce and glanced at Essix. The falcon sat at a small arch window high in the basement, looking too dignified to fly farther into the room.

Still holding the torch, Rollan moved to the base of the stairs. With his free hand, he removed his dagger from his belt. "Mind taking a look?" he asked Essix. "It's probably Meilin and Abeke, but we'd better check just to be sure."

The bird screeched, then took flight through the room and up the winding metal staircase. Although now empty, the Howling House was still a scary place to be. Every time the wind blew outside, the windows rattled, making Rollan flinch. The four walls surrounding them were covered with scratches and splatters of red. Rollan didn't care to speculate on the source of the stains.

Rollan watched Essix as she soared back into the basement. She perched on the wooden chandelier in the middle of the space and began pecking at something—probably an insect snack.

"She flew down here," Rollan heard Meilin say. A few moments later, she and Abeke descended the stairs into the basement.

"What happened to you all?" Rollan asked, holding the torch so he could get a better view of them. "How did you get covered with all that ash?"

Meilin brushed the soot from her shoulder. "We ran into a little trouble, but we were able to handle it. Any luck with finding anything on the Wildcat's Claw?"

"Not yet, but we haven't been searching long." He pointed them toward an untouched stack of books covered in dust and cobwebs. "You can start with those. The others are farther back, looking through, like, a thousand scrolls."

Meilin cautiously approached the books. "Are you sure there aren't any spiders in there?"

Rollan smiled. "If you see one, just pretend it's a big, hairy mouse."

She huffed in reply, but picked up one of the scrolls. Abeke took a large book beside it.

Rollan removed his cloak and returned to his book. It was cold outside, but all the torches were making the basement stuffy. The brown cloak was heavy and rough, nothing like his green cloak. He hadn't wanted to part with it, but after Abeke's speech last night about secrets, Rollan knew he couldn't continue traveling with the cloak and hiding it from his friends. He and

Worthy had decided to store it in Dawson's cottage for now, underneath one of the loose floorboards. Hopefully, once they'd found all the gifts and rescued the Greencloaks, Rollan could return for it.

He wondered if Tarik would have done the same thing, had he still been with them.

Rollan finished paging through the book, then picked up an equally large and equally boring journal. He had to keep shaking his head in order to stay awake.

But then his eyes flashed open.

"I think I found something!" Rollan said. He'd discovered a full-page illustration of a large, bearded warrior and a black wildcat. The warrior's arms were thick as tree trunks. The fur of a wild stag covered his shoulders, torso, and legs, and his metal helmet was adorned with two sharp, ivory tusks. In his hands, he carried a large sword, poised and ready to strike.

As intimidating as the warrior was, the wildcat was even more ferocious. It stood in a crouch, claws bared and mouth curled into a snarl, waiting to pounce. Somehow, the ink in the drawing made it seem as though the wildcat's muscles rippled underneath its fur, right there on the page. Its yellow eyes peered at Rollan, as if it were trying to stare him down.

Rollan finally peeled his eyes away from the drawing, as the others surrounded him. "That's it!" Worthy said. "That's the picture I remember seeing."

Worthy took the journal from him. Rollan didn't try to stop him. "The warrior is named Gransfen the Giant," Worthy said. "The wildcat's name is Wilco."

"Like the enchanted forest?" Conor asked. "Wilcoskov?"

Worthy nodded. "Yes, I believe so." He flipped the page and continued reading, his finger tracing along each word. "This looks like a brief retelling of the history of Gransfen and Wilco. They lived a long time ago, back before there were even Greencloaks." Worthy looked up from the journal. "Hey, maybe the Trunswicks are somehow related to him. I think I had a cousin named Grant . . . maybe he was named after him. I should ask Dawson about—"

"Let me see that," Conor said, taking the book from Worthy. "You can come back later to research your family history—after we find the Wildcat's Claw."

Conor began reading the book—slowly. He'd hardly been able to read when Rollan had first met him, but he had worked hard at it—even studying during their travels—and had improved greatly.

"According to this, Gransfen was from the far north. Somewhere close to the shores of Arctica." Conor kept reading. "A band of warriors called the Crimson Raiders attacked his village, taking most of the food the villagers had harvested for the long winter. The leader of the Crimson Raiders demanded that the village swear loyalty to them and hand over their firstborn sons to their order—if not, they would destroy everything. Gransfen, the first and only son of the local blacksmith, was weak, scrawny, and sickly. In order to prove they were serious, the Crimson Raiders pulled Gransfen from his home, stripped him of all his furs, and cast him into the wilderness to starve and freeze to death. He returned three weeks later, alive and well, riding on the back of the largest wildcat anyone had ever seen. The wildcat roared so loudly that the village gates disintegrated, like a charred log turning to ash. Then the wildcat fought the raiders, snapping their swords in her jaws like they were twigs in a steel trap."

"That's amazing," Rollan said. He had to admit, Wilco sounded pretty awesome—maybe even more powerful than the gila monster.

Conor turned the page. "After freeing the village, Gransfen and Wilco spent the rest of their lives fighting against the Crimson Raiders and any other threats to ancient Eura. The book compares the black wildcat to other legendary animals from across Erdas, especially in Amaya, Nilo, and Zhong. Their strength only paled in comparison to the Great Beasts themselves. Like Wilco, some of these spirit animals and their human partners had powerful items that they used to defend their homes. The book names four: the Wildcat's Claw, the Heart of the Land, Stormspeaker, and the Dragon's Eye. All four were gifted to the Greencloaks after the fall of the Devourer."

"Those are the other two gifts!" Abeke said. "Stormspeaker and the Dragon's Eye."

"Jump ahead," Anka said. "Does it say what happened to them?"

Conor flipped to the end of the entry and began reading again. "No, but it does say that after years of glorious battle, Gransfen and Wilco were buried at the base of a waterfall in the very forest where Gransfen first summoned the wildcat." Conor perked up, his eyes gleaming. "*Even the famous Greencloaks revered the pair,*" he read haltingly. "*Shortly after the war, a traveling Greencloak visited the tomb to honor the wildcat and the hero.*" Conor flipped to the next page, but it was blank. "That's it," he said.

"I'm guessing that Greencloak was doing more than just paying respects," Rollan said. "They must have been hiding the sword."

"But why?" Meilin asked. "This has been bothering me for a while now. If these gifts are so powerful, why didn't the Greencloaks keep them and use them to defend Erdas? The Heart of the Land has saved us twice now. We could have used that power against the Conquerors, but Olvan held back."

Rollan frowned. "It is a little strange. Especially since they're supposed to be these big symbols of togetherness. Why spread them all out and keep them hidden?"

Anka's color shifted slightly. Rollan caught a glimpse of a thoughtful expression before she disappeared again. "The Greencloaks have always been tight-lipped about forbidden knowledge," she said. "Perhaps there's more to the gifts than it seems, and they wanted to keep those secrets from getting out."

"Until now," Conor said. "Whatever his reasons, Olvan needs us to retrieve the gifts."

"Great," Worthy moaned. "Are we really going to Wilcoskov?"

"What's wrong with that?" Abeke asked. "Is it dangerous?"

"Worse," Worthy said. "It's enchanted. Full of old magic. No one enters that place anymore, not even hunters."

Meilin shrugged. "Gransfen did."

"Gransfen was the most noble warrior that Eura has ever known," Worthy said. "No offense, but even you aren't in his league, Meilin. None of us are."

"The book says that a Greencloak entered the forest," Abeke offered.

"But it doesn't say that he left, does it?" Worthy said.

Rollan arched his eyebrow. "Worthy, are you really that scared?"

Behind his mask, Worthy's eyes were solemn as he looked at Rollan. "I am. And if you knew any better, you'd be scared, too."

Conor closed the book. "I'm scared, too. I grew up hearing all the horror stories about Wilcoskov. But if the Wildcat's Claw is there, then that's where we have to go." He looked at Worthy. "Are you with us?"

Worthy scowled, but eventually nodded. "Fine, I'm in. But don't say I didn't warn you."

Rollan decided to tag along with Meilin and Abeke on the way back to Dawson's cottage. After being cooped up in the basement, he wanted to run along the rooftops, feeling the breeze in his hair. On the way, they filled him in on the trouble they'd run into at Trunswick Castle.

"We'll have Dawson go back to release them as soon as we leave," Meilin said once they neared the cottage. Rollan noticed a few candles burning by the window. He hoped that Dawson hadn't stayed up waiting for them. Running a town like Trunswick couldn't be easy. The kid needed all the rest he could get.

"People will eventually figure out that Dawson was the one helping us," Abeke said. "I hope he doesn't get into too much trouble."

"He's a smart kid," Rollan said, his hand on the door. "I'm sure he'll find a way to talk himself out of it."

He opened it, and froze.

"Or maybe not," Rollan mumbled.

Three members of the militia stood in front of him, their crossbows aimed right at his chest. Another woman stood a few feet away, a saber in her hand.

"Don't even think about calling your spirit animals," the woman said. "Just come in, nice and quiet."

Rollan, Meilin, and Abeke slowly entered the room.

"Close the door," the woman said.

Rollan shook his head. "It gets really warm in here, with so many people," he said. "But I'd be happy to close the door once you all leave." He didn't know how far away Anka and the others were, but he hoped that with the door open, they would see the trouble that they were in before walking into the same trap.

"I'm sorry that I couldn't warn you," Dawson said. "The captain got here a few minutes ago."

"The young earl almost had us fooled," the woman said. "But then my men found the strangest item in his bedroom, hidden underneath the floorboards." She held the tattered green cloak up high, then let it unravel to the ground.

Rollan didn't miss a beat. "Dawson, you're a Greencloak! You should have told us—"

"Save it," the woman snapped. She walked over to the three men holding crossbows. They looked pretty banged up, with ripped clothes and ash in their hair. One could barely hold his weapon—the wrist of his non-firing hand was wrapped in a thick bandage. "Are these the kids you saw running through the streets?"

"Yes, Captain," the oldest one said. "The two girls. The boy wasn't with them."

Rollan realized these must have been the men who chased Meilin and Abeke. Either they had escaped their bonds, or someone had found them and released them.

Meilin shook her head. "I told you that you should have shot them," she whispered to Abeke.

"Why are you here?" the captain asked. "We've had enough of your kind in our town. Conquerors, Greencloaks, Oathbound, and everyone else. We just want to live our lives in peace." The woman almost sounded like she was pleading. "Why can't you just leave us alone?"

"Just put the weapons down, and we'll be gone before morning," Abeke said. She glanced at the three men with the crossbows.

The captain shook her head. "The Oathbound will be back by then with more men. I don't know how, but they could tell you were here. Their leader, Cordelia the Kind, threatened to ransack only *half* the town if we turned you over upon their return."

"She calls *that* kind?" Rollan shook his head. "And I thought Wikam the Just was misnamed."

"Please consider what you're proposing," Dawson said to the woman. "You'd be a fool to trust the Oathbound over the Greencloaks. Surely you've heard the rumors about these bounty hunters dressed in black. They don't care who or what they destroy. They don't care about anything in their path. They only care about catching their target, no matter what stands in their way."

"Yes, I'm a fool," the captain said, turning her gaze to Dawson. "I'm a fool for thinking you were better than your father. You're a liar, just like him. Do you plan to steal from us, too?"

"I am *not* my father," Dawson said, his jaw taut. Beside him, Rumfuss snorted and tapped on the floor with his hoofed feet. "Shylene, I asked you to organize the militia because you are brave and fair. You were one of the only people to speak out against my father. You always know the difference between right and wrong." He took a step toward her. "Trust your instincts," he said. "You know I'm telling the truth."

"Look at your men," Rollan added. "Can't you tell from their faces? They know we don't mean them any harm."

The captain glanced at her men. Their expressions were much more conflicted than hers. "It's true, Captain," the bearded one finally said. "They could have killed us, but didn't. And they fixed up Sully's arm and everything."

The captain shook her head. "How can you trust them?" she asked. "How can you trust *any* of them? These outsiders care nothing for your lives or your families."

"Then don't trust them," a voice said. "Trust me."

Rollan turned. Slowly, Worthy faded into view, like a fog taking human shape. The men gasped.

"What type of trickery is this?" the oldest man asked, his arms shaking as he pointed his crossbow at Worthy. "Stay back, monster!"

Worthy flinched. Rollan wasn't sure if the man had called him a monster because of the way Worthy had materialized in front of them, or because of how the Redcloak looked. Either way, it wasn't a compliment.

"I'm not a monster," Worthy said. "I'm one of you. At least, I used to be." He took a cautious step inside the cottage.

"Stay where you are," the captain warned, swinging her weapon toward him. Unlike her men, she didn't seem the least bit intimidated. "Who are you?"

"I'm called Worthy," he said. He reached behind his head and unfastened his mask. "But before, I was known by another name."

The woman's eyes narrowed as she took in Worthy's unmasked face. She blinked a few times. "Devin Trunswick?" she asked, her voice softer. "Is that you? What happened?"

"That isn't important." He took another step forward. "So you do remember me. Do you also remember the last time we saw each other?"

She nodded, still taking Worthy in. "At the center of the square," she said. "I'd been locked in the stocks for three days with barely any water. I didn't know how much longer I could last. But you . . . you stirred the crowd and started a riot. The townsfolk overtook the guards, then freed me. We marched to the castle after that and burned it down. I would be dead if not for you. The earl would probably still be in power as well." She pointed her sword at Rollan and the others. "You're working with these Greencloaks?"

"I am," Worthy said. "I trust them with my life."

The woman took a deep breath. "Then I trust them as well," she said. "Lower your weapons," she said to her men. "These Greencloaks mean us no harm." She sheathed her sword then turned to Dawson. "I'm sorry about what I said."

He was already waving her off. "Don't worry about it. You were only doing your duty. No one is above question in Trunswick, including me."

"I should apologize as well," Rollan said to Abeke and Meilin. "I'm sorry for bringing the cloak with me. I just couldn't part with it yet."

Meilin patted his shoulder. "I know," she said. "But no more secrets, okay?"

Rollan nodded. "No more. Complete honesty from now on."

Meilin raised an eyebrow. "About everything?"

Rollan could feel the heat rising to his neck. "Well, almost everything. I do have a reputation to protect and all." He looked at Worthy. "And speaking of truths—who would have guessed that Worthy was actually telling the truth about saving that woman? Maybe he's not so bad after all."

THE ENCHANTED FOREST

MEILIN'S HORSE NEIGHED AND STOMPED AT THE STIFF ground. She rubbed on its neck, trying to calm it. The animal didn't like carrying her, that was for certain. He was a field animal, more suited for pulling a plow than racing into battle, but riding was better than walking.

Meilin readjusted the sword at her side so it wouldn't interfere with her new, royal blue uniform. In addition to providing horses, Shylene, the captain of the militia, had issued each of them a Trunswick militia tunic. The journey to Wilcoskov would have taken weeks if they'd been forced to travel by foot under the cover of night. But by pretending to be part of the militia, they hoped to be able to travel during they day without attracting too much attention.

Meilin squeezed her knees around the horse, motioning him forward. She trotted over to the three militiamen—the same men who had chased her and Abeke the night before. Even with the tumble they'd taken through the floor, they seemed to be in good shape, thanks to Jhi's healing powers.

"Thank you for the horse and the clothes," she said. "But you don't have to travel with us. It could be dangerous."

"Captain's orders," the bearded one said. Meilin had learned that his name was Albert and that he was a pig farmer. "The villagers to the north know our faces. You'll be questioned less if you're seen traveling with us."

"Thank you," Meilin said again. It seemed too much of a risk—these simple townsfolk risking their lives to help them. But Meilin reminded herself that the people of Trunswick had much to lose as well if the Greencloaks weren't successful.

The others slowly climbed onto their horses. Anka looked the strangest of them all, wearing her blue tunic, plainly in sight. She still carried Meilin's old quarterstaff.

Rollan was the last to mount his horse. He almost fell off a few times, but he eventually made it onto the saddle. "Are you guys sure that you don't want to walk? It's probably safer."

Meilin rolled her eyes. Even after all this time, Rollan still wasn't comfortable on horseback.

They passed the city walls just as the sun peeked over the horizon. Now that it was easier to see, Meilin noticed that the flags flying above the city walls displayed the image of Rumfuss the Boar. The last time she'd visited, the flags glorified Elda, the black wildcat with whom Worthy had been unnaturally bonded.

Meilin slowed down and joined Worthy at the rear of the group. "Did you enjoy being home?"

"It's always good to see my brother," Worthy said.

"But this isn't really home anymore." He nodded toward the men at the front of the group. They were talking with Conor, laughing about some shared story between them. "Did you see how they looked at me? Did you hear what they said? They've made a point of steering clear of me."

"It's just because they aren't used to the way you look," Meilin said. "Give it time."

He gave a weak laugh. "That would be fine, if it were only that. But my face and claws aren't the only reasons why they keep avoiding me. Dawson was right—the old Devin Trunswick was a real bully. Take Sully, for instance," he said, nodding toward the youngest of the militiamen. "His sister was jailed in the Howling House for a week, all because my father and I didn't like the way she looked at us when we passed by one day. And Albert and his hog farm? I used to take my dogs hunting on his land once a fortnight, and wouldn't even pay Albert when my hounds slaughtered one of his pigs."

"Have you tried apologizing?" Meilin asked.

He seemed hopeful. "Do you think that would really work?"

Meilin shrugged. "I don't know. But it doesn't hurt to try."

They continued riding all day, not stopping until it was almost dark. While Conor, Rollan, and Abeke prepared their meal, Meilin took Anka and the other militiamen to a clearing to work on some fighting techniques.

"The key to good fighting is good footwork," Meilin said, standing before them. Four arm-length strips of cloth were draped over her shoulder. "If you stand with your feet too close together, you run the risk of losing your balance and falling in a fight. If your feet are too apart, you won't be able to move fast enough to counter your opponent's attacks." She tossed each of them one of the strips. "Tie these between your ankles, and let's get started."

She spent the next hour working on their footwork, having each of them attack and parry. Then she had them pair up and face off against each other. Meilin was worried that Anka would struggle against the older Albert, but she held her own, even causing Albert to trip and fall a few times.

Once dinner was ready, the three men untied their cloths from their ankles and rushed to the campfire. Anka stayed behind.

"You're not hungry?" Meilin asked, picking up the discarded strips from the ground.

"I'll eat in a little bit," Anka said, twirling her quarterstaff like Meilin had taught her. "I want to practice a little more first."

Meilin pulled out her sword. "I'm ready whenever you are."

As Anka and Meilin began to circle each other, Toey, Anka's chameleon, scampered down her leg and hid in her boot. "You're getting pretty good with that quarterstaff," Meilin said, before lunging.

Anka blocked her blade, then swung the other end of the staff at Meilin. Meilin ducked and then rolled out of the way. "Very good," Meilin continued, getting to her feet.

"Thanks. I've been studying how you move," Anka said. Now she became the aggressor, swinging and lunging at Meilin. Meilin blocked each strike, then leaped onto a tree branch, out of reach of Anka's staff.

"Let's try again," Meilin said, peering down at Anka from the safety of her tree. "But this time, use your spirit animal."

Anka leaned against the quarterstaff and wiped her brow. "Are you sure? That doesn't seem fair."

"In a real battle for life and death, you shouldn't worry about what is and isn't fair," Meilin replied, swinging out of the tree. "We're partnered with our spirit animals for a reason. Use Toey's strengths to help you."

Anka nodded, then began to fade from view. Meilin spun in a circle, waiting for Anka to strike. Finally, Meilin heard the familiar swoosh of the quarterstaff swinging through the air, and stepped to the side just as it hit the ground. She stomped down, pinning the staff between her boot and the dirt, then performed a spinning roundhouse kick, knocking it loose from Anka's grip. Slowly, it came into view.

Meilin grinned. "Come on, Anka. You can show yourself. The fight is over."

"Not yet," Anka said. "Would you stop fighting just because you didn't have a weapon?"

Meilin faced the direction that she thought the voice was coming from. "I don't want to hurt you," she said. "Seriously, you should—"

With an *oomph*, Meilin found herself on the ground, the wind momentarily knocked out of her chest. She flipped back into a fighting stance and scanned the area. She still couldn't see Anka. Smirking, she began to run in a circle, dragging her boot heels into the dry ground. She was creating a small dust storm.

Finally, she saw something waver before her. Then Anka coughed. "There you are," Meilin said, running after her.

Anka took off toward the same tree that Meilin had leaped into moments before. She reached the trunk, then quickly scampered up the bark before disappearing into the leaves. Meilin stopped and placed her hands on her hips. She'd never seen Anka move that quickly before. She wondered if her sudden increase in speed was thanks to her spirit animal.

"Let's call this one a draw," Meilin said, still searching the tree. "I'm tired, and our dinner is getting cold. The only thing worse than hot grub stew is cold grub stew."

"Deal," a voice said behind her.

Meilin spun around to find Anka standing there with the quarterstaff in her hand. Its end hovered underneath Meilin's chin, ready to strike. A sly smile sat on the now visible Anka's face.

"Remind me not to spar with you again without Jhi's help," Meilin said, pushing the staff away from her. "How did you get out of the tree and around me without me seeing or hearing you?"

Anka shrugged. "You've been good at fighting your whole life. I've been good at hiding." They began walking toward the campsite. "I can teach you if you'd like. Show you how to move better without being seen."

Meilin shook Anka's hand. "It's a deal."

Anka smiled at her once more. "I'm glad fate brought us together, Meilin. You're almost like the sister I never had."

Meilin grinned as well. *Sister.* That had a nice ring to it.

Meilin continued to train Anka and the militia whenever they camped for the night. Worthy even helped out with their training a couple times. The men were still wary of him, but they didn't keep their distance like they had at the beginning of the trip. Meilin hoped that they were making progress toward becoming friends. Or if not friends, she at least hoped that the men could understand that the past was the past, and that Worthy was now a different person.

The days had grown colder the farther north they traveled. The winds strengthened as well, bringing freezing rain, then sleet and snow. She was glad that they'd come equipped with wool packs. That would help keep their clothes and food dry.

The weather was indeed brutal, almost as bad as when they'd trekked through Arctica in search of Suka the Polar Bear. If they were lucky, the conditions would also slow the Oathbound. Using Essix's powers, Rollan had caught sight of them two days prior. They, too, were headed north.

The group paused at the edge of a large river. Fog hugged the ground, covering the frozen soil and rocky banks. Across from them stood the enchanted forest, Wilcoskov.

"Why do they call it enchanted?" Abeke asked, sliding off her horse.

"I'm not really sure," Worthy said. "There used to be rumors that an ancient order lived in the forest. They practiced dark magic, using the bones of children in their potions." He shrugged. "At least, that's what my tutors used to tell me when I misbehaved."

"According to my brothers, the forest is filled with the ghosts of the Crimson Raiders," Conor added. "As punishment for their crimes against Eura, the royal family banished the warriors to the forest. They supposedly froze to death within hours, but their tortured spirits remained tied to the forest for all eternity."

"Knowing the Greencloaks, they could have started the rumor about the forest being enchanted," Meilin said. "They probably assumed it would be a good way for people to stay out and away from Gransfen's grave."

"There's only one way to find out for sure," Abeke said, leading her horse to the militiamen. "This is as far as you all go," Abeke said to Albert. "And you can take these horses with you. It'll be easier for us to travel without them."

"That's the first good news I've heard all week," Rollan said, sliding off his own mount. He landed on the ground with a thud and the horse nickered. It sounded as if it was laughing at him.

Worthy slipped off his tunic and handed it to Albert. "Do me a favor," he said. "Keep an eye out for my brother, will you? He can be a little hardheaded."

"Sure thing." Albert took the tunic. "Good luck, my lor—uh, Devin—I mean, Worthy." He extended his hand to Worthy, and the boy eagerly took it for a handshake. "And stop by my home the next time you're in town. My kids would love to hear more about your adventures."

Worthy smiled at the man. As Meilin watched him, she realized that, for the first time on their journey, he wasn't wearing his mask.

After the militiamen rode off, Conor began cutting some fallen logs in order to make a raft. With all of them working together, it only took a few minutes to collect the logs and lace them together.

Using a thick branch, Conor navigated them across the water. "This'll probably be frozen solid in a few weeks," Conor said, pushing the branch into the river bottom. "Good thing we didn't try to swim across. We'd probably freeze to death."

Once on the other side, they quickly scampered up the bank. "This isn't a forest," Rollan said. "It's more like a graveyard. A place where trees go to die."

Meilin didn't want to agree with Rollan, but he was right. Wilcoskov was very creepy. The fog covering the ground was so thick it looked like they were stepping through rain clouds. Ahead of them, the naked trees stretched to the sky, with snow capping each of the bare branches. The wind blew through the skeletal trees, making a howling, almost unnatural sound.

Before entering the forest, they called forth their spirit animals, including Jhi. Meilin knew they'd need as much help as possible to get through the tangled maze. Essix flew ahead in search of the waterfall, while the others followed Briggan, Uraza, and Jhi.

They traveled for what seemed like hours. Meilin was sure that they were just walking in circles—each tree looked the same—though the animals never appeared to be confused. Dead, stiff moss covered all the trees, creating silver curtains cascading from the sky. Gnarled roots and thick, twisted branches blocked them from all sides, making the journey that much slower. They couldn't make it ten paces without some-one tripping on something, or being sideswiped by thorns or huge burrs. Somehow, the wind seemed to blow from all sides all at the same time, never giving them a break from the frigid chill.

Finally, Essix returned, landing on a tree in front of the other animals. After squawking a few times, she took flight again. The other animals continued moving forward.

"I think that means we're going in the right direc-tion," Rollan said, his teeth chattering.

They kept moving, walking through lunchtime. The wet, cold air had somehow made it through Meilin's leather boots and wool socks, the chill digging deeper with every step. She walked beside Jhi, in the hopes that the animal would keep her warm. Rollan had mocked her at first . . . before finally huddling against the giant panda as well.

Sometime later, Meilin jolted to a stop as a foul stench hit her nose.

"That is dis-gust-ing," Rollan said, covering his mouth. "And I thought this place couldn't get any worse."

"Over here," Conor said. Using his ax blade, he jut-ted toward an animal carcass. "I think this is what's causing the smell." He turned it over, and a new wave of foulness hit them. "Yep, this is it."

"What type of animal is that?" Meilin asked, step-ping closer. The huge creature had been ripped open, with half its flank already devoured. She could still see the claw and teeth marks in its skin. As she circled it, trying to get a better look, she noticed another gap-ing hole in the animal. It looked as if it had been ripped apart. Two broken tusks protruded from its snout. What remained of its gray, coarse fur was matted with dried blood.

"There are two more carcasses over here," Worthy said. "They smell like Rollan's feet."

"Ha-ha," Rollan said dryly.

"Is it native to Eura?" Anka asked Conor.

He shrugged. "I've never seen it before."

"Me neither," Worthy said. "It looks like some type of huge hog. Or perhaps a boar."

"I think we should leave," Abeke said. She had drawn her bow and nocked an arrow, and was cautiously spinning around in place. Uraza stood beside her, crouched low to the ground, almost hidden by the fog. "Those carcasses were killed recently."

Meilin took a step backward, and stumbled. Waving the fog away, she saw a line of deep, massive paw tracks.

"We're in some animal's lair," Abeke continued. "We need to leave before it returns."

Then Briggan growled. "Too late," Conor said, his gloved hands tightly gripping the handle of his ax. "Briggan senses something. I do, too."

Then they heard a branch snap. And then another after that.

"This way," Anka said, moving toward a group of trees. "I'll hide us."

As quietly as they could, they made their way to Anka. After a second, they turned silver and brown, blending into the dying trees and moss behind them.

All the while, the sounds of crunching leaves and tree limbs grew closer. Something howled. Something close.

"Don't even breathe," Abeke whispered.

Slowly, five brown bears appeared out of the fog. As they growled at one another, Meilin could feel Rollan flinch beside her. The bears were gigantic—at least as large as Jhi—with thick coarse fur covering their hulking bodies.

The bears lumbered farther into their lair. The largest of them sniffed at one of the carcasses, then let out a wailing roar. Frothy drool dripped from its jaw and onto the ground. On the other side of her, Meilin could hear Worthy's ragged breaths, and she knew it wasn't from the cold.

A second, smaller bear approached the largest one, sniffing the air. The animals turned toward Meilin and the others. They growled, spewing more drool across the frozen ground.

"I think they can see us," Worthy whispered.

The three other bears joined the first two. They all began to paw at the ground, letting off a succession of grunts.

"Maybe they're just pawing at the ground to stay warm," Rollan offered.

Then, letting off a deafening roar, the bears charged toward the trees. *Their* trees.

"Run!" Abeke screamed.

They took off, thrashing through the woods. The bears followed close behind. The entire forest seemed to shake thanks to the bears thundering paws. At first, Meilin had been worried that Jhi would be too slow, but the great panda was easily outpacing her, only pausing to make sure *she* was keeping up.

"We can't run like this forever," Rollan said. "Let's take to the trees."

"The branches are too low," Conor said. "They might be able to climb after us."

"No, over there!" Worthy said, pointing to a large tall evergreen to their right. Its lower branches had already been stripped by something, leaving nothing but exposed, clawed bark until halfway up the tree.

"Aren't you worried about what made those marks on that tree?" Rollan asked.

"I'll worry about that later," Worthy replied as he extracted his claws and began climbing the tree. Anka quickly climbed up behind him.

"Jhi, can you help the rest of them up?" Meilin asked. She glanced behind her. The bears were still charging, their wails ringing through the forest. "Abeke first. Then she can give us cover."

Jhi lumbered to the base of the tree, then held out her paws. Abeke nodded, called Uraza back in passive, then took off toward the panda. She leaped into the panda's outstretched paws. Jhi flung her high into the air, past Worthy and Anka. Abeke grabbed on to a branch and pulled herself up. As soon as she was sitting, she whipped an arrow from her quiver and began firing at the bears. The arrows found their mark but did not puncture the bears' thick hides. However, they at least slowed down.

Meilin was the last into the tree. As soon as she grabbed a branch, she called Jhi back to her. The black-and-white mark appeared on the back of her hand just as the bears reached the base of the tree.

The animals raked their claws over the tree trunk, but were too large to climb it. Then they rammed the tree, over and over, causing snow and small branches to rain down from above. Abeke almost fell after one attack, but Conor was able to catch her and pull her back onto the branch at the last second.

"Thanks," Abeke said. She slipped her bow back over her shoulder. "No point in wasting any more arrows."

"So now what are we supposed to do?" Anka asked.

Meilin shrugged. "We wait. And hope that the tree outlasts the bears."

THE WATERFALL

THE BEARS RAMMED THE TREE FOR ALMOST AN HOUR. The trunk bent and sighed with each attack, but didn't break. Eventually, the bears tired of this, and their attacks slowly dwindled. But instead of leaving, they curled up around the tree, content to wait the humans out. It seemed the bears knew Conor and the others couldn't remain in there forever.

Conor wasn't sure how long they ultimately stayed in the tree. Day had turned to night before the bears finally disappeared back into the fog. But even then, they waited a full two hours before venturing down, just to be safe.

Conor decided to go down first. Once he reached the ground, he released Briggan. The wolf stepped forward and sniffed the air. After a few seconds, he seemed satisfied that the threat had disappeared and returned to Conor's side.

"Come on down," Conor said. "I think it's safe."

"Hopefully the Oathbound will run into those bears as well," Rollan said, sliding down the tree.

"Has Essix seen them?" Conor asked.

Rollan shook his head. "That's what worries me. They're no longer on the road to the forest. So either they turned around, or they're already here and hidden from Essix's view."

"Keep your eyes open, Uraza," Abeke said. "We need to be on the lookout for both animals and Oathbound."

"And ghosts," Worthy mumbled.

Following their spirit animals, they continued on in what they hoped was the direction of the waterfall. They didn't dare light a torch—they didn't want to draw any unwelcome attention. Using Briggan's senses, Conor took the lead, trying to help navigate them past any unseen obstacles. Worthy only tripped twice. Conor took this as a positive.

"We should stop for the night," Anka finally said. "It's getting too difficult to see. Plus, I don't want to stumble into another den of those wild bears by accident."

They all agreed. Finding a large outcropping of boulders, the team hastily made camp. Conor offered to keep first watch. He knew he wouldn't be able to sleep anyway.

Conor had heard stories about the great Euran wildcat all his life. She was second only to Briggan in fame. Many towns and villages had flown her likeness on their official banners and flags, in the hopes that she would bring good luck—such as protection from wild animals or a good harvest. Conor couldn't believe he was actually close to seeing the grave of the real beast. He didn't like all the fighting and politics associated with being a Greencloak, but he loved the adventure and the thrill of discovering new things. Even with everything that had happened, he didn't want to go back to his old life as a shepherd and servant boy.

Once morning came, the group packed up and continued through the forest. As the day wore on, the roar of falling water grew louder. The sound seemed to propel them forward, encouraging them to scamper through the forest at a quicker pace.

Finally, the forest opened up, revealing that they were standing at the top of a huge valley. They gasped at the sight. Sunlight reflected brilliantly off the water below, forcing them to shield their eyes. To their left, a large thundering waterfall cascaded down a fragmented cliff face, creating a thick, white mist where it joined with a swirling pool. The rushing waters churned within the cove; Conor could make out huge, jagged rocks and massive boulders poking through the surface. The water seemed to thrash around the small bay before continuing downstream along a twisting path to deeper parts of the forest.

Conor cupped his hands over his eyes to get a better look at the valley. There, at the banks of the river, were blooming red and yellow flowers. He rubbed his eyes, just to be sure they were working properly, then looked again. There even appeared to be fruit trees down at the bottom of the falls, lush with green leaves. How could that be? How could anything grow in this environment, with all that snow and ice?

Then he realized that the valley *had* no snow and ice. The landscape of ice and dead trees faded away about a quarter of the way from the base of the valley, replaced with wide trees and other wildlife.

"Guys, it's not snowing down there," he said. "See the plants and flowers?"

They all leaned forward to take a closer look. "That's impossible," Abeke said. She shook a small, ice-covered branch beside her, dumping freshly fallen snow to the ground. "How can it be freezing up here, and a paradise down below?"

"Some rumors say that the black wildcat breathed fire when she was really mad," Worthy said. "When she hissed and spat, she'd be liable start forest fires. Maybe some of that heat is still around."

Meilin rolled her eyes. "Or more than likely, we're close to a geyser or fault line that keeps that area warm."

"Maybe that's why they called it an enchanted forest," Anka said. "It would have certainly appeared magical to people not used to sights such as this."

"I don't care what they called it, and I don't care why it's warm," Rollan said. "I just want to get down there so I can feel my fingers and toes again."

They slowly made their way down into the valley, traversing roots and outcroppings of boulders. As they continued down, Conor began removing layers of his warm clothes. By the time they reached the bottom, they had all shed their heavy fur coats. The rumble of the waterfall was so loud that they had to yell in order to hear one another.

"I'm betting there's a cave somewhere behind the falls!" Meilin bellowed. "But what's the best way to get to it?"

Abeke picked up a small piece of wood and tossed it into the water. It bobbed up and down in a frenzy as it was quickly swept downstream. "We won't be able to swim to it. There's no way we could fight against that current."

Conor was relieved to hear her say that. While he could make do in the water, he wasn't the best swimmer. Worthy seemed to be just as relieved by Abeke's observation.

"Maybe there's another way around," Rollan said. "Here comes Essix now, to save the day." Then Rollan grew still, and Conor knew he was slipping into the falcon's mind.

Conor looked up to see Essix's brown wings stretched wide. She slowly spiraled down into the valley, soaring over the team's heads. Tucking her wings into herself, she dove into the waterfall. For a moment, Conor was worried that the strong, pummeling water would send her crashing into the rocks below. But then Essix emerged from the other side, not a feather out of place.

"Yeah, it looks like there's an entrance back there," Rollan said, shaking his head. "There's a small ledge that leads to a cave behind the waterfall. It's narrow, but I think we can make it." He pointed to a rocky land ramp leading to the cliff wall. "That's the way up."

They followed Rollan as he shrugged off his pack. "Be careful," he said, reaching the face of the cliff a few moments later. "The ledge is covered with moss and lichen, and slick from all the water."

The rest of them removed their packs, only taking what was essential. Meilin hesitated after removing her pack, almost as if she was going to pull something from it, but left it on the ground with the others. Conor offered Briggan a leftover piece of jerky from that morning's breakfast, then called the wolf into passive state. He didn't want to take the chance of Briggan loosing his footing and falling into the river. Briggan was strong, but that current would have been too much for even him to swim against.

One by one, they climbed onto the narrow ledge, their backs pressed against the rough, uneven cliff face. Conor's toes hung over the edge. Now was not a great time to have large feet.

"I wish we had some rope to tie ourselves together with," Meilin said. "Maybe we could use some of the vines from the forest."

"We'll be fine," Rollan said, slowly edging along. "Just don't look down."

Of course, Conor chose right then to glance below him. His stomach twisted and churned just as much as the river beneath them.

Conor was halfway across when they heard a rumbling sound.

"What is that?" Anka asked. "More bears?"

"No, it's much closer," Meilin said. "It almost sounds like it's coming from the—duck!"

Conor covered his face as a wave of bats streamed from behind the waterfall. They were small, but loud—their shrieks even blocked out the roaring water.

"Keep moving forward," Abeke yelled, shielding her face with her arm. "We have to make it to the cave."

Just then, another sharp scream pierced the sky. But this wasn't an animal. It was a distinctly human voice.

"Rollan!" Meilin yelled.

Conor opened his eyes to see Rollan flailing below them, his arms outstretched as he plummeted toward the bubbling water. Rollan was heading right for one of the largest–and sharpest–of the boulders.

Maybe Rollan sensed what was ahead. Ceasing his flailing, he pulled himself into a ball. Then, when the time was right, he kicked out against the cliff and dove cleanly into the water. By pushing himself away from the wall, he was able to avoid the largest of the rocks.

"Yay!" Conor cheered. "I thought he was a goner."

"It's not over yet," Anka yelled. "Look!"

To their horror, Rollan was thrashing around the water, fighting against the current, but he was losing steam.

"Hold on to something, Rollan!" Abeke yelled.

Rollan turned, trying to grab a boulder, but he slipped past it and continued down the river. He pivoted again, trying to grasp another rock, but instead smashed into it. Rollan was visibly shaken by the impact, his head rolling around on his neck.

"I'm going in," Meilin said. She pressed her hands against the rock wall, preparing to launch herself off.

"No, you can't," Abeke said. "You're not strong enough!"

Meilin was furiously shaking her head. "He'll drown if I don't go."

"No, you'll both drown," Worthy said. "But I won't." And with that, Worthy let off a ferocious howl and leaped off the cliff. With his red cloak billowing behind him, he almost looked like he was flying as he dove into the water.

Worthy disappeared into the frothy haze, and for a second, no one saw him. Then he emerged, spitting water as he did.

"Hold on, Rollan!" Conor yelled. "Keep fighting! Worthy's coming for you!"

Worthy paused for long enough to get his bearings, then sped toward Rollan, his arms and legs propelling him through the water. He caught the boy just before he was about to get pulled into the twisting current and dragged farther into the forest. Worthy handed Rollan something. It looked like a black vine. And then, very slowly, Worthy turned his body and powered through the white-capped current. Conor realized he was holding his breath as he watched his friends battle back to dry land.

Finally, Worthy and Rollan reached the bank. Conor and the others crawled off the ledge and rushed to them.

Jhi appeared with a flash by Rollan's side before Meilin had even reached him. The panda licked him a few times, but he waved her away. "I'm fine," he said. "Just need . . . to catch . . . my breath." He pointed a shaky finger at Worthy. "Help him."

Worthy lay sprawled out on his back, his mask slightly askew. "I. Hate. Water," he said as the panda licked his face. "But I think I hate panda spit more."

"Worthy, that was amazing!" Conor said, kneeling beside his friend. Worthy had a few scratches, but otherwise seemed okay. "I can't believe you did that!"

"It was also very brave," Meilin said, much more quietly. She placed her hand on the Redcloak's shoulder. "Thank you."

"Yeah, Worthy, thanks for giving me a hand back there," Rollan said, still lying on his back. He paused, his lips twisting into a smile, then added, "Or I guess I should say, thanks for giving me a tail."

Worthy finally stood up. "Not another word," he warned, straightening his mask. "Or I'll throw you back in myself." But then he placed his hands on his hips in a heroic pose. "And you're welcome."

"Do you want to change clothes?" Abeke asked, nodding toward their discarded packs. "Are you cold?"

"I'll be fine," Worthy said. "Plus, there's no way I'm taking off this cloak."

They all fell silent for a second. Conor was sure that they were all thinking about their abandoned green cloaks.

Meilin helped Rollan to sit up. "Your cloak is ripped," she said, fingering the brown fabric. "You should change into something dry."

"I'll be fine," Rollan said. "It's not even that cold down here."

"No, seriously." Meilin walked to her pack, then carried it over to Rollan. She slowly rummaged through it. "I think I have something you'd be more comfortable in."

She pulled out his green cloak.

For a moment, Rollan seemed speechless. He took the cloak from her, running his hands along it. Then he brought it to his nose, smelling it to confirm it was his. "But I thought it was too dangerous to keep this," he finally said.

"I know," Meilin replied. "But we're Greencloaks. We shouldn't be ashamed of who we are." She helped unfasten the brown cloak from around his neck, then tossed it aside. "I think we'd all feel a little better with a reminder of Tarik on this journey. We all miss him, too."

12

BOND TOKENS

WORTHY HAD NO IDEA WHY HE LEAPED OFF THE CLIFF to save Rollan. Worthy hated water. And now his beautiful red cloak was drenched, making it twice as heavy.

As he wrung out the fabric, he told himself that he'd jumped to save the Heart of the Land tied around Rollan's neck, but he knew he was lying to himself. As much as he didn't want to admit it, these Greencloaks were growing on him. He actually liked Rollan, bad jokes and all.

Prior to joining the Redcloaks, he'd always had trouble making friends. When he was younger, other kids had played with him only because they were forced to by their parents in order to gain favor with his father. Similarly, when he was a Conqueror, the only reason that Zerif put up with him was because of his father's importance and hefty monetary donations.

But these four—Conor, Abeke, Meilin, and Rollan— they genuinely cared for one another. They liked spending time together. And now, he liked spending time with them, too. He even liked Anka, when he remembered she was there.

Once he and Rollan had rested from their dip in the water, they tried to scale the cliff again. This time, they tied themselves to one another using black vines found in the valley forest. Rollan looked as if he was going to make another joke about Worthy's tail, but one look from him made Rollan reconsider.

Worthy took the lead this time. With his claws, he had a better chance of holding on to the cliff if someone fell and tried to drag them all down.

"How much farther?" Anka yelled as they passed behind the waterfall.

"Almost there," Worthy called back. Once behind the waterfall, the ledge widened, making it big enough for him to walk without hugging the wall. Very little sunlight was able to stream through the falls. The ledge was dark, so he waited for a moment to let his eyes adjust. Eventually, he noticed that the overhang grew even wider as it approached what looked like the cave entrance.

He froze once he was at the opening. "Whoa," he murmured.

Before Worthy stood the largest statue he'd ever seen— and being the son of the former Earl of Trunswick, he'd seen plenty. The sculpture was similar to the illustration of Gransfen and the mighty Wilco from the journal they'd read at the Howling House. Carved from what looked like pure black obsidian, Gransfen held the famed Wildcat's Claw in his hands, pointing it at an unknown enemy. Wilco, nearly as large as the man, stood on her hind legs, her claws ready to maul their unseen foe.

At first, Worthy thought the statue had been built all the way to the top of the cave. But after noting the small boulders and crushed rocks lying at the base, he looked again. The entrance had begun to cave in. It was only the statue—literally, Gransfen's broad shoulders—that kept the cave mouth open.

"Don't touch it," Anka said as the others joined them at the statue. "We don't want to accidentally cause a collapse. There's no telling how long we'd be trapped in here."

They slowly stepped past the statue. Conor released Briggan. The wolf scratched at the rocky ground then stepped farther into the cave, following Conor. The others released their animals as well, and a splash announced that Essix had soared through the waterfall. She landed on Rollan's shoulder and shook her feathers out, dousing him with water.

With her beak, she lifted up a small edge of Rollan's green cloak.

"Like it?" he asked.

The gyrfalcon squawked a reply. Rollan nodded. "Yeah, me too," he said, following the others into the cave.

As the cavern narrowed, Conor pulled a torch from his waistband, and he and Briggan took the lead at the front. Worthy covered the rear, turning around every few minutes to make sure that they weren't being followed. Now that his eyes were fully adjusted to the dark, he didn't need as much light to see. But with the falls still roaring in their ears, he was afraid he wouldn't hear someone sneaking up on them until it was too late.

The cave was a series of long, narrow tunnels, each connected end on end, and each growing smaller as they moved farther into the cliffside. Briggan and Uraza growled as their feet slipped on loose pebbles. Glancing above, Worthy noticed more bats. Thankfully, this bunch didn't seem interested in waking up and attacking them.

"Yuck," Conor said from up ahead. "I walked right into a spiderweb." Then a second later, he added, "Sorry Meilin. I meant to say a mouse web."

"Thanks," she replied, with a little tremble in her voice. She placed her hand on Jhi, who barely fit through the narrowing spaces. Jhi rubbed her muzzle against Meilin, then gave her a friendly lick on the arm. Worthy couldn't help but smile. Meilin was the finest warrior he'd ever met. How could someone so ferocious be afraid of spiders?

The long, dark cave dead-ended into a huge expanse. But it wasn't a natural cavern—it looked like it had been hand-carved. Worthy ran his hands along the smooth wall. Something caught his attention. Someone—or some*thing*—had etched small intersecting ridges into the wall.

"Ouch!" Rollan yelled, falling over as Essix took flight from his arm. "There's something in the middle of the room. It looks like a big, rectangular rock. Conor, can you bring the torch over here so I can get a better look?"

"Wait, try to light this first," Abeke said, pulling a dusty, half-burned torch off the wall. "I think it will still catch."

"There's another torch over there," Meilin called out.

Conor quickly lit the torches with a flint and some oil, illuminating the room.

Worthy stepped back to get a better view of the wall. It wasn't just random ridges. It was a drawing. No, a language. It looked like etchings of runes—ancient letters used by long-gone Euran civilizations.

"Can you read it?" Meilin asked him.

He shook his head. "I don't think so." Worthy had been forced to learn a lot of languages, but he didn't remember any of his tutors showing him writing like this. The more he stared at it, however, the more he realized that some of the symbols were familiar.

"Guys, come take a look at this," Rollan said.

Worthy and Meilin joined the others. Two matching, equally large slabs of rock sat in the middle of the room. They looked to be made of solid stone, but they didn't match the rocky makeup of the cavern walls.

"I think it's the same type of stone the statue was chiseled from," Worthy said, kneeling to get a closer look. He placed his hands on the tablet, then pulled it back. The room was warm, but the slabs were as cold as the forest above them. "They're freezing," he said. "How is that possible?"

"And how did they even get them through the cave?" Rollan asked. "Those things are massive. They're way too large to fit through all those winding tunnels and way too heavy to carry."

Meilin took her torch and circled the slate. "I think there are hinges on this side," she said.

"I see some, too," Anka said from the other side. "It kind of looks like a door."

"But how do you open it?" Rollan asked. "There aren't any handles."

"Look around," Abeke said, "There must be a switch or lever somewhere that will trigger it open."

While the others started inspecting the cavern walls, pressing into the rock in the hope that they'd find a secret button, Worthy returned to the runes.

"I think this might be a message," he said. "But it's old. I'm going to try to decipher it."

The others searched the entire room while Worthy sat cross-legged in front of the wall. Using his claws, he wrote out possible translations into the rocky ground, but nothing seemed to make sense.

"Making any progress?" Anka asked, appearing beside him. Worthy jumped and let out a small scream.

"Sorry, didn't mean to sneak up on you." She pointed to the wall. "Any luck?"

He shrugged, then looked back at the words he'd drawn on the ground. "The closest I've come is: *Each day must end, but the mighty shall rise again under a volcano's roar.*"

"That makes no sense," Rollan said, pausing beside them.

Worthy snorted. "You want to give it a try?"

Abeke aimed an arrow toward a natural hollow in the ceiling. She released it, hitting the hole spot-on, but nothing happened. "Essix, do you mind retrieving my arrow?" she asked the falcon. She returned her bow to her shoulder. "Keep working on the translation, Worthy," she said. "I have faith in you. It could be the instructions on how to open the doors."

"Or it could be a warning that we should leave them shut." But even as he said it, Worthy was sitting back down to study the markings.

The rest of the Greencloaks searched the entire room again. Rollan even tried jumping on the doors, but all he accomplished was slipping and hurting his other foot.

He sighed as Jhi slowly licked his ankle. "This is pointless," he said. "Maybe there's another cave we missed. Or a switch outside of the room."

"Worthy, can you repeat the message?" Abeke asked, shooting another arrow at the ceiling. "Maybe we'll have better luck if we work together."

Worthy sighed, then repeated the message: *"Each day must end, but the mighty shall rise again under a volcano's roar."*

Abeke walked over to read Worthy's translation. "The first part reminds me of an old saying from my village. When someone dies, the elders sometimes say that the deceased's 'sun has set.' Their day has ended. It's a poetic way of talking about death." She glanced at the door. "I think the message is saying that Gransfen and Wilco are behind those doors. They're waiting to rise again."

Meilin snapped up, suddenly alert. "And on the boat, on the way from Amaya, Worthy said the wildcat's roar was as loud as an erupting volcano."

"One thousand erupting volcanoes," Worthy corrected.

"Yes, yes," she said. "My point is, you learned that as a kid, right? That can't be a coincidence. It must mean something important."

"I was thinking the same," Rollan said. "When volcanoes blow up, they're like earthquakes, right?" He slipped his hand inside his shirt and pulled out the

Heart of the Land. "Maybe I can try using the gila monster's earthquake power."

"Are you daft?" Worthy asked. "You'd cause a cave-in. Did you bash your head in when you fell into the water?"

"I said *maybe*," Rollan stressed, returning the amulet to the safety of his shirt. "I'm just throwing out options. We have to do something."

"Volcanoes also spew lava when they erupt," Meilin said. "Fire. Heat." She held up the torch in her hands, inspecting its flame. "Maybe we should heat up the doors. You said those slabs were cold, right? Maybe warmth will trigger the doors to open."

"So . . . if we set the doors on fire, they'll open up, and Gransfen and Wilco will rise again?" Conor asked.

"Just to be clear, I'm not exactly sure that my translation is correct," Worthy said. "For all we know, an actual volcano could be waiting for us on the other side."

Meilin stepped forward. Her torch illuminated her face as she walked to the center of the room. Her hair was damp from sweat, and her skin was covered in grime from the cavern walls. "Only one way to find out."

Meilin tossed the torch onto the slabs. It bounced twice before coming to a stop. Conor and Abeke followed her lead, pitching their torches on the black slates as well.

At first nothing happened.

Then thick gray smoke began to seep out through the seams between the doors.

"It's the volcano!" Worthy yelled.

"Enough about the volcano," Meilin said. "Look, something's happening."

The doors in the floor had begun to change color, quickly shifting from their dark ink-black color to a fiery orange-red hue. There was a large hiss and then a pop. The doors slowly began to creak open.

More smoke spilled out as the doors opened up. Worthy could see what looked like long stone columns rising up from below, pushing the doors open from the inside. With a thud, they slammed against the floor, shaking the room. Small rocks fell from above, but the room didn't collapse.

Something was rising out of the hole in the floor.

Worthy watched as a large, gleaming box slowly emerged up into the cavern. It was the same deep black color as the slabs, chiseled with careful precision. All across the edges, scenes of a great cat performing heroic acts glittered, carved in relief into the stone. Once completely out of the ground, the black box creaked to a halt. The smoke thinned out, and the red doors returned to their dark color.

"It's a coffin," Anka said. "It must be the final resting place of Gransfen and the wildcat."

Now that it was all the way out, they could see dull yellow and red jewels covering the rectangular container on all sides. Conor picked up one of the still-lit torches and held it over the coffin. The jewels lit up like stars in the midnight sky.

Worthy noticed something else gleaming on top of the box. Whatever it was, it was covered with soot and dirt. Worthy blew across the top, revealing a silver blade. A thick leather-wrapped hilt shone through the soot, and a large yellow stone, cut into an oval shape, was embedded in the center of the hilt.

The Wildcat's Claw.

Anka started to step toward it, but Rollan stopped her. "I think Conor or Worthy should pick it up," he said. "It's a Euran gift. Someone from this land should activate it."

Conor looked at Worthy. "You deciphered the code," he said. "You should take it."

Worthy shook his head. "Are you sure?"

Abeke placed her hand on his shoulder. "Don't be afraid," she said.

It wasn't that Worthy was afraid. It was more like, he didn't know if he was actually worthy enough to hold the sword. Gransfen and Wilco had been the protectors of an entire land. He was just a kid in a white mask and red cloak trying to make up for his past mistakes.

"Do it, Worthy," Conor said. "I believe in you. We all do."

Worthy nodded, his eyes stinging behind his mask. Then he reached out and grabbed the hilt. The leather hadn't been used in aeons, but it was supple, like it had just been oiled. He lifted the sword and was surprised by how light it was, given its size. It was easily the largest, longest sword he'd ever wielded, but it felt as weightless as a training foil.

He adjusted his grip on the sword and took a few swipes. The metal almost sang as it sliced through the dusty, smoky air.

"Look here," Conor said, pointing. "There's a small incision at the base of the tomb. I think you're supposed to place the sword here."

Worthy began sliding the sword into the opening. The sword sang again as its steel blade scraped against the black stone. Worthy felt it lock in place, and slowly let go.

The room began to rumble, and more rocks and debris fell from the ceiling. The hilt of the sword began to glow. Worthy took a closer look. He realized it wasn't the metal underneath the leather that was glowing. It was the yellow jewel at the center of the sword. If the gems on the tomb were stars, then the jewel on the sword was the shining sun, beaming brightly enough to blind them all.

Smoke began to surround them, this time seemingly coming from all sides of the room, as the jewel shone brighter and brighter. Then the jewel flashed, causing Worthy to cover his eyes.

When he opened them, he saw the image of a man beginning to form from the smoke. Well, not a man. More like a giant. Worthy had to look up to see his face. The man's beard hung to his belt buckle. His face was rough and weathered, similar to the cliff they had traversed, but there was a lightness in his eyes.

"Gransfen," Worthy whispered. He stole a glance at the others. They all stood at attention, with their backs straight and arms taut. Worthy adjusted his body so he looked the same.

"Is he talking yet?" Meilin whispered. "We can't hear him if he is."

"No," Worthy said. "Nothing—"

Who is mighty enough to raise the Wildcat's Claw? Who is brave enough to wake me from my eternal slumber? Who is—

Gransfen's eyes became pinholes in the smoke. *Is this the Great Briggan? And Uraza and Jhi?* He looked up at the nook in the ceiling where Essix rested. *This is most unexpected.*

The man's words felt like they were pounding in Worthy's head—like a thousand erupting volcanoes. He looked back at the others, waiting for one of them to respond, but only Conor's expression had changed, his mouth now hanging open.

No matter. Again, who raised my sword? Was it you? Gransfen had leveled a smoky finger at Worthy, who stood closest to the blade.

Worthy gulped, then nodded. "Yes, I raised the sword." He puffed his chest out and placed his hands on his hips. Hopefully that made him look more commanding. "I am Worthy, of the Redcloaks."

Gransfen peered at him, a puzzled look coming to his face. *What are you? You do not look Euran. Those eyes . . . I would recognize the gaze of a wildcat anywhere.*

"I am of Euran blood," Worthy said. Slowly, he removed his mask, setting it on the cavern floor at his feet. "But I am also more. I'm part human . . . and part wildcat."

That seemed to please the giant man. *The wildcat is a noble beast. Ferocious. Loyal.* Lowering his hand, Gransfen placed his palm against the stone coffin. *Wilco died protecting me. She died protecting Eura. I was never the same without her. My heart shattered like ice against rock.* He shook his head. *I hoped that death would ease my pain. It has not.*

"What's he saying?" Rollan asked.

"He's talking about Wilco," Conor said.

I sense a strange presence. He leveled his gaze on Rollan. *A bond token is here, one that's different from ours.*

"Rollan, show him the amulet," Worthy said. "I think he wants to see the Heart of the Land."

Rollan quickly pulled the amulet from off his neck. As he held it up, the amber stone began to glow. It pulsed in tandem with the yellow jewel of the Wildcat's Claw.

Gransfen let off a loud, booming sigh. *Who is its owner?*

"A legendary warrior, like you," Conor said. "These were gifted to our . . . our army, but they were hidden away for a reason before we could use them. Do you know why?"

Perhaps because of their strength. Bond tokens are powerful, but also deadly when placed in the wrong hands. Gransfen ran his hand over his long, flowing beard. *Long ago, Wilco and I protected Eura from the greatest of dangers. But there were some threats so treacherous that even we could not defeat them alone. There were men who used distrust and division to turn leaders into sheep. To transform the just into the wicked, the sure-footed into timid fools. These men would use fear and hatred to create entire armies. They would channel rage and anger into weapons of destruction and death.*

Harmony, and only harmony, could defeat a danger like this.

The ultimate harmony between human and animal. The ultimate trust.

It was Wilco who led me to Suka the Great Polar Bear. There in the frozen wasteland of Arctica, towering above me, Suka showed me the crystal talisman hanging from her claw. Holding it in her massive paws, she displayed its might, leveling a snowcapped mountain one hundred paces away with the slightest wave of her arms. I held out my arms, waiting to receive the gift of such power.

But she refused to turn over her talisman. Instead, she instructed me to create one of my own. My bond token, like her crystal bear talisman, would amplify Wilco's powers. It would be a weapon capable of defeating the largest of armies. If used properly, Wilco and I would be unstoppable.

But it would take true trust, Suka cautioned. One shred of doubt between either Wilco or myself would rip the mystic bonds holding us together. We would be lost to each other forever, both consumed by a cloud of despair that would only be soothed by death itself. Others had tried, she warned. Others stronger and braver than us. Many had failed and had been henceforth doomed to eternal madness.

And even if we were successful, the Great Polar Bear warned, we would have to guard our token for the rest of our lives. The token's power could be tapped by anyone, not just me. Not just another of the Marked. It could be harnessed whether Wilco was in passive state or not. It could be used by anyone, anywhere, at any time. Its power would live on forever, even after we had departed this world. But if it were destroyed during our lifetimes, we would immediately perish as well, as it was an extension of our bond.

I remember looking at Wilco, my partner. My friend. Her yellow eyes gleamed. She roared into the white, frozen abyss. She was ready. So was I.

I drew my sword, forged with my own two hands, and performed the ritual. I could feel the power flowing between us, rolling like a mist over a swampy land, and I watched as it folded itself into my blade. The yellow stone, a gift from my mother, began to shine like it harnessed the fervor of an everlasting sun.

And then, it was done. The mighty Wildcat's Claw had been forged anew. And with it, we cut down our enemies and feasted on their burned, charred corpses.

Worthy cringed as he said this. That part didn't seem too appealing at all.

Gransfen looked down at the team. *Those that stand before me, are you unified?*

"Say yes," Conor said to the others.

"Yes," they all mumbled.

Are you worthy of these gifts?

"Yes," they said again, watching Conor for the clues.

And are you willing to die to protect one another, and these gifts, even if it leads to your deaths?

"Yes," they said.

Then take the Wildcat's Claw, and fight for all of Erdas. Use its power, and let the mighty wildcat roar once more.

Worthy nodded. "We will," he said as Gransfen's image began to fade away. "I promise." He wrapped his fingers around the sword and pulled it back out of the cleft.

"Yikes!" Rollan said as the ground began to shake. The stone coffin was receding back underground, the air alive with a soft hiss as steam and smoke once again surrounded them. Then the large slate doors turned fire-red again and began to creak shut, seemingly without anything acting on them to cause them to move.

Once the doors slammed closed, they returned to their black color. The room fell silent. Save for the sword in Worthy's hands, there was no clue that anything magical had happened at all.

"Did you guys hear any of what he said?" Worthy asked.

Rollan shook his head. "It was the same way in Amaya. Only people from the land of the gift can hear the hero's echo."

"The gifts are called bond tokens," Worthy said. "At least, I think that's what he said. He was kind of loud and boomy. My ears are still ringing a little."

"Bond tokens?" Abeke frowned. "I've never heard of that before."

"Actually, you have," Conor said. "They're kind of like the talismans from the Great Beasts." He quickly explained what Gransfen had told him and Worthy about the power of the bond tokens. "And they can be used by anyone, whether you're Marked or not."

"You said we could make these ourselves, right?" Meilin asked. "If that's the case, then why haven't the Greencloaks ever created them? They would be helpful in battle, especially when our spirit animals were still in passive state."

"The Greencloaks have always been secretive about information they consider dangerous," Anka reminded them. "Like the source of the bonding Nectar and the location of Stetriol." She ran a small finger along her chameleon's bumpy back. "Perhaps that's why the nations lost their faith in them."

"They were only doing what was right for Erdas," Abeke said.

"Tell that to all the people in Stetriol and everywhere else that got the bonding sickness, just because the Greencloaks weren't around to personally administer the Nectar," Rollan said. His words were hard and bitter. "Think of all the people who drank the Bile because it was the only way to cure their bonding sickness."

Worthy knew that Rollan was talking about his own mother. Unlike Worthy, Rollan's mother had taken the Bile for noble reasons. To try to cure herself, so she could find the son she'd been forced to abandon in Amaya.

"There are other reasons to not share that information," Conor said. "If a bond token is destroyed, both the human and the animal partner *die*. Think what would have happened if the Conquerors had known that during the war."

"Maybe that's why the Great Beasts were so protective about their talismans," Rollan said. "I would be, too, if I knew someone could come along and smash it, wiping me from existence."

"Yes, and that's *if* the technique to create one even worked in the first place," Worthy added. He had sat down and was using his cloak to shine the sword. "Gransfen said it required absolute trust between partners. All it would take was one thread of self-doubt to doom both the human and the animal. The bond would break between them. Shattered. Forever." He looked up. "Isn't that right, Conor?"

Conor was looking down at his own spirit animal,

as were Meilin and Abeke. Even Rollan seemed to have a faraway look.

"I've had my bond broken before," Abeke finally said. "It isn't something that I'd hope for again."

"Yes," Worthy said. The blade was sharp, and he'd accidentally sliced a hole in his cloak. "But as long as there's complete trust between you and the animal—"

"We should move out," Meilin said, rising. "It will be dark soon."

Worthy looked as his friends, clearly troubled. Perhaps their bonds weren't as strong as he thought they were.

Briggan growled. A second later, so did Uraza.

Worthy stood up. He'd heard it, too. The crunch of pebbles against boot heels. The scrape of metal against rocky walls.

"Get ready, Greencloaks," Worthy whispered. "We're about to have company."

"It must be the Oathbound," Meilin said. "Any clue how many?"

Worthy tried to count all the different footsteps but quickly lost count. "A lot," he finally said. He looked at the others as their faces became stern. "So now what are we supposed to do?"

Abeke slipped her bow off and pulled an arrow from a quiver. "Now we fight."

THE BATTLE

ABEKE INSTRUCTED CONOR AND MEILIN TO BLOW OUT the torches. Thanks to Briggan's powers, Conor's eyes immediately adjusted to the dark. Abeke had crouched at the opening of the cavern, her body low to the ground. "I'll take out as many as I can. But they'll break through eventually."

Conor pulled out his ax and bounced on his toes. Briggan seemed frisky as well, ready for action. "Try to be patient," he said to the Great Wolf. "Our time will come soon enough."

"Out of all the places to face off, it had to be deep down in an underground cave," Rollan said, patting the amulet underneath his shirt. "That means no earthquake powers for us."

Meilin turned to Worthy. "You seem to know all about the wildcat," she said. "Maybe you can figure out how to activate the Claw's powers."

"It would be great if it could magically transport people to safety." Rollan pulled a dagger from his belt, then another from his boot. "That would be really helpful right about now."

"Quiet," scolded Abeke. "They're almost here."

"Perhaps I should take the gifts," Anka whispered to Conor and Rollan. "If you all can lure enough of the Oathbound out of the passage and here into this room, I may be able to use my powers to slip by undetected."

Conor and Rollan looked at each other. "That's probably a good idea," Conor finally said. "Our first priority has to be protecting the bond tokens."

"Yeah, but a very close second priority should be getting out of this alive," Rollan added.

Worthy seemed to hesitate as he handed the sword to Anka. Conor had to admit, he looked at ease carrying it. It had made him seem more imposing. More inspiring.

"Do you want me to take the Heart of the Land as well?" Anka asked Rollan as the Wildcat's Claw disappeared from sight. "I can smuggle it out, too."

Rollan paused as well before shaking his head. "We should split them up, just in case." He held up his arm, signaling Essix. "You'd better take this," he said to the falcon, sliding the leather strap holding the amulet from around his neck. He tied it around one of the bird's talons. "Now don't get any fancy, heroic ideas," he said to Essix. "If this turns ugly, you fly that amulet to safety as fast as you can."

"*If* this turns ugly?" Meilin said. "We're talking about an army of soldiers against six. It's going to get ugly."

"Meilin, honesty is a currency that doesn't have to be spent all in one place," Rollan said.

"I can see them," Abeke whispered. "Be ready. They're going to charge as soon as I start firing."

Abeke closed one eye as she brought the bowstring to her cheek. She waited and waited . . . and then released the arrow. A second later, an Oathbound soldier screamed in agony.

"Charge!" someone yelled from the tunnel. The footsteps turned into a thunderous roar.

That must have woken up the bats, because all of a sudden Conor heard them shrieking. Moments later, they spilled into the room in an enormous cloud, their black wings filling all the available space in the cavern.

Conor swiped at the bats with his ax, knocking two to the ground. Briggan snatched another out of the air, shaking it with his massive jaws before flinging it against the wall.

"I can't see!" Abeke said. "They're blocking my aim." She quickly fired off three more arrows, then ducked as the Oathbound returned fire.

"Look alive, Greencloaks," she said, retreating from the opening. "Here they come!"

The first wave of Oathbound stormed into the cavern. Many had arrows stuck in their arms and shoulders. Spirit animals rushed in with them.

Worthy yowled as he leaped toward a group of three. He quickly knocked two of them against the wall, but the other pierced Worthy's side, cutting him through his thick red cloak. Worthy yelled, clawing the Oathbound across the arm. The man released a boa constrictor, which quickly wrapped itself around Worthy's neck.

"Hold on, Worthy! We're coming!" Tapping into Briggan's strength, Conor flew across the room, his boots barely touching the ground as he ran. He sliced one of the Oathbound with his ax as he passed by, then crashed into the group of soldiers surrounding Worthy, knocking them to the cavern floor. Rolling to his feet,

Conor quickly sidestepped a swinging broadsword, then blocked a billy club aimed at his face.

"Ouch!" he yelled, looking down. A lynx had grabbed hold of his leg, right above his boot, sinking its teeth deep into Conor's flesh.

Before he could shout for help, Briggan appeared, grabbing the animal by the neck. With a loud growl, it ripped the lynx away from Conor.

"Are you okay?" Conor asked, pulling Worthy to his feet. "Did the snake bite you?"

"No, more like I bit it," Worthy said as he spat out a few yellow-green scales. "And I don't care what anyone says. It doesn't taste like chicken."

More Oathbound rushed toward them. "Back to back," he said to Worthy. "You take the eight on your side. I'll take these six."

"And how exactly is that fair?" Worthy asked, swiping at the men.

Across the room, Meilin and Rollan fought off another group of Oathbound. Meilin's sword kept four of them at bay while Jhi reared up on her hind legs and swatted the men down. Rollan used both his daggers to simultaneously block and attack the Oathbound. Rollan had a cut against his cheek, but it didn't look deep enough to slow him.

Conor didn't see Essix in the fray. He hoped that meant the falcon had gotten to safety.

"Oh, no!" Worthy yelled. "Anka's down!"

Conor looked in the direction that Worthy had pointed. Anka, no longer invisible, was slumped against the cavern wall, a stream of blood trickling down her face. The Wildcat's Claw had fallen from her grasp and lay untouched on the floor.

A woman with a ruby-red sword rushed toward Anka. The woman's brown braided hair flopped behind her as she ran.

"She's going for Anka," Conor said. "Come on!"

Conor and Worthy took off, pushing their way through the Oathbound warriors to try to reach Anka and the Wildcat's Claw first. A man with a longsword lunged at Worthy, but Conor jumped in the way, blocking the blade with his ax hilt before it reached Worthy. The warrior then smiled as a meerkat leaped from his back onto Conor's face.

Conor spun around, trying to keep the animal away from his eyes. The meerkat was small, but its claws were sharp. Conor screamed as it raked its paw across his forehead.

"Conor!" Worthy yelled.

"Forget about me," he yelled, dropping to the ground. "Protect Anka and the sword!" Conor rolled around, trying to dislodge the animal from his face. Although his eyes were closed, he could hear Briggan nearby, squaring off with the man with the longsword.

Finally, Conor slammed his head against the ground. It was like being hit in the face with a brick, but the maneuver successfully dislodged the animal. Rising to his feet, Conor kicked the meerkat across the room. Just before it was going to land, Uraza leaped into the air, snagging the beast.

"Bomilo!" the warrior shrieked, running after Uraza.

Conor turned to see that Worthy had made it to the Wildcat's Claw. He knelt before it, but hadn't yet picked it up.

A few paces away, the tall woman warrior stood with a garrison of soldiers behind her. The woman had placed the tip of her ruby-red sword right underneath the unconscious Anka's chin.

She snapped her fingers, and one of the men behind her raised a concave horn to his lips. A low wail echoed through the room. The Oathbound immediately stopped fighting.

"Put down your weapons," the woman said, moving her blade closer to Anka's throat. "This battle is over."

14

THE WILDCAT'S ROAR

A BEKE WAS JUST ABOUT TO RELEASE ANOTHER ARROW when a loud horn reverberated throughout the room. The Oathbound warriors advancing toward her immediately stopped and began to pull back.

Why are they retreating? she wondered. *Have we won?* She looked at Uraza. The Great Leopard's purple irises showed the same confusion that must have been present on Abeke's face.

Her bow still in her hand, Abeke searched the cave for the others. Meilin and Rollan stood side by side, their weapons lowering slowly. Conor was in the process of setting his ax down on the ground.

Then she saw the woman. Tall and regal, she towered over Anka, a long red sword pointed at the Greencloak's throat. Abeke worried that the woman had killed her, but then she noticed Anka stirring a little.

"Perhaps you didn't hear me," the woman said, keeping her blade at Anka's neck while meeting Abeke's gaze. "Either lower your bow, or your friend loses her life."

Abeke stared at the woman, looking for any signs of bluffing or weakness. Gaudy rings circled each of the Oathbound's fingers, serving as a stark contrast to her otherwise drab uniform. The woman sneered, then moved the blade closer to Anka. The tip pierced Anka's skin, drawing a single drop of blood.

Abeke slowly released the tension in her bow. As she placed it on the ground, she noticed Worthy unbuttoning his cloak.

"Just proving that I'm unarmed," he said as the cloak floated to the ground. She wasn't sure, but she thought she saw the glint of a silver blade right before the red cloak fell over it.

Worthy then spun in a circle, just to prove his point. His black tail waved behind him.

"My, aren't you a peculiar one?" the woman said. "Perhaps I'll spare you after all. I could add you to my collection. Or perhaps I'll make you my pet."

"My name is Worthy," he said defiantly. "Who are you?"

"I am Cordelia the Kind," she said. "Haven't you heard of me?"

Rollan snorted. "The trappers told us about you. You don't sound very kind to me."

One of the men pushed Rollan in the back, almost causing him to trip.

"Kindness, like beauty and power, is all a measure of perspective." Removing the sword from Anka's throat, she walked over to Worthy. "I *could* use this blade to sever your friend's tail from his body," she said. She smiled, then raised her foot and jammed it onto his black tail, grinding it into the rocky ground. Worthy howled, baring his teeth, but didn't move to strike the woman.

"But wasn't that a kinder gesture?" Cordelia said, batting her eyelashes.

"Leave him alone," Abeke said. Beside her, Uraza growled.

Cordelia turned her attention back to Abeke. "Greencloaks, put your spirit animals away. Now." Once they'd all complied—and Briggan, Jhi, and Uraza disappeared into flashes of color—the woman turned to a group of warriors to her right. "Bring them here," the woman said. "But be careful. None of them are to be underestimated. If they're bold enough to kill the emperor, think what they will do to you."

Abeke jerked away from one of the warriors as he tried to grab her elbow. Holding her head high, she marched to join the others beside Worthy. "We didn't kill the emperor."

"Then why did you run?" Cordelia asked. "Why not remain at the Citadel and face trial?"

"The Greencloaks do not answer to bounty hunters like you," Abeke said. "We heard about how you threatened all the towns in Eura during your search for us." She shook her head. "Why did you terrorize those people? They've done nothing wrong."

"Harboring fugitives and withholding information is a crime," she said. "I was merely giving them incentive to cooperate." She returned her sword to her belt. "And don't worry, I only burned the homes of half those trappers. I'd threatened to destroy *all* their belongings if they failed me. Again, my kindness has no bounds."

"The Oathbound aren't a sovereign military," Conor said. "You're mercenaries. You don't have the right to arrest people."

"People are afraid. Scared of the Greencloak army that has already destroyed much of this land. They want us here to protect them. Who else is mighty enough to stand against the evil Greencloaks?" She twisted a ring around her finger. "The queen herself has welcomed our assistance in any way, especially when we deliver you to her in six wooden coffins."

Abeke thought about what Gransfen had said. People, when afraid, would follow anyone. Even a group as twisted as the Oathbound were proving to be. And worse, people would do it willingly.

"But because I am so kind, here's what I propose," Cordelia continued. "If you turn over the two gifts you've located, I'll allow three of you to live. You can spend the rest of your lives rotting in a cell."

"We don't have them," Worthy said. "Essix took them both and escaped."

"And you'll never catch her," Rollan added. "Both the gifts are long gone by now."

Cordelia paused to consider this. Abeke realized that the woman didn't know what the Wildcat's Claw looked like. It was the only thing working to their advantage.

Cordelia spun on her heels, then marched to Anka. She knelt in front of her, her lips snarling. "If that is true, why were you trying to escape?" she asked Anka. "Do you have the gifts? Or are you just a coward that hides and runs instead of fighting?"

It only lasted for a moment, but Anka's eyes flashed to the ground, toward Worthy's feet.

"Silly Greencloak," Cordelia said. "Your eyes have already betrayed you." Cordelia rose, then started to move toward Worthy.

Just as she reached him, Worthy thrust his fist into the sky. The Oathbound drew their weapons, but Cordelia held up her hand.

"I have the Heart of the Land," Worthy said, his fist clamped shut. "Move another step, and I'll start an earthquake and bring this entire cave down."

"I don't believe you," she said. "You would kill everyone in here."

"That's better than letting you have the gifts," Worthy said.

Cordelia spun another of the gold rings around her finger. "Nothing is in your hand," she said. "You're lying."

"I guess there's only one way to find out," Worthy replied. His yellow eyes stared back at Cordelia, unblinking.

"Actually, there are two ways," she said. She nodded toward one of the Oathbound who was standing beside her. "Shoot him. Let's see what falls from his hand when his warm body hits the ground."

Worthy's eyes widened as the soldier raised his crossbow. "Fine. You want it? Take it!" He reached back and hurled his hand forward.

Cordelia and every other Oathbound spun and stared, searching for the invisible amulet as it tumbled through the air.

"Liar," she said after a moment, turning back around. "I knew—"

She stopped. Worthy's red cloak was draped across his arm. He held the Wildcat's Claw in his other hand.

"My, my, you really are full of surprises, aren't you?" She shook her head. "That's a nice sword. But how long do you think you'll last with it?" She took the crossbow from the Oathbound holding it and aimed it at Worthy's chest. "My kindness has run its course. Now, where are the gifts? I won't ask again."

Worthy tightened his grip on the sword and took a step forward, placing himself between the Greencloaks and the Oathbound. "Cordelia, let me introduce you to the Wildcat's Claw." As he said the name, the jeweled hilt began to glow, driving all the darkness from the cavern. "Not every gift is as small as an amulet."

She didn't lower her weapon. "Hand it over and I'll let you live." Then she paused. "From what I remember of Euran history, the famed black wildcat didn't have special armor powers like the Amayan gila monster. It couldn't stop arrows in midair."

"That's right," he said. "But haven't you heard of the wildcat's *ROAR*?"

As he said the words, the yellow jewel began to smoke. The sword vibrated in Worthy's hands as it gave off a low, deep rumble. There was a loud boom, and then fire spewed from the jewel like a geyser turned on its side, the orange flames leaping horizontally across the room. The Oathbound nearest to Worthy were immediately set ablaze. Cordelia dropped her crossbow and rolled out of the way before getting singed herself.

Worthy waved the sword at the Oathbound, pushing them back, then looked behind him at Abeke and the others. "Don't just stand there and stare. Attack!"

Abeke rolled, plucking one of her arrows off the ground, and stabbed it in the nearest Oathbound's thigh. As another rushed toward her, she released Uraza in a flash. The leopard raced across the space between her and the attacker, flinging herself at the man. The warrior tried to hit the animal with a quarter-staff, but Uraza easily dodged, and grabbed the end of the weapon as it bobbled in the air. She yanked it from him, then swiped at the man again, slicing his arm.

The Oathbound solider retreated, but two more arrived in his place. Abeke picked up Cordelia's abandoned crossbow. Not as good as a bow, but it would do. She quickly fired a bolt into one of the men attacking Uraza, then turned and smashed the weapon into another Oathbound's head.

"Head for the mouth of the cave!" Worthy yelled, the Wildcat's Claw still breathing out fire. "I'll hold them off!"

"I've got Anka," Conor said, helping her to her feet. "Let's go."

Rollan and Meilin took the lead, punching and stabbing any soldier that got in their way. Meilin's attacks were almost poetic, the girl spinning and kicking in a way that exuded grace and control. Rollan was more rough around the edges, slicing and thrusting like a madman, but it was just as effective.

After using the last of her bolts, Abeke flung the crossbow to the side and grabbed a bow and quiver of arrows from an unconscious soldier. As they slowly fought their way forward, she continued to collect and fire arrows at approaching soldiers. Once out of the cave, they rushed toward the waterfall.

"Great," Rollan said. "Don't look now, but there are more Oathbound waiting for us."

Indeed, another set of soldiers had trickled in. Abeke fired an arrow at one of them. He fell as it struck his leg, but there were just too many to stop them all.

"Hold on," Worthy said. He moved to the front and held the sword steadily before him. Again, fire sprung from the hilt, causing the men to scatter backward.

"Keep moving," Meilin said. "They're catching up behind us."

Abeke turned to look. Sure enough, Cordelia and her men were quickly rushing through the tunnel, swords drawn and crossbows level.

They reached the mouth of the cave. The tall black-carved statue stood just as they'd left it, its shoulders still bearing the crumbling ceiling. Oathbound now stood on two sides of them. The waterfall rushed just behind the forward group.

"We're flanked on both sides!" Worthy said, turning the fire back toward Cordelia's group. She and the approaching Oathbound retreated farther down the tunnel, but the others were now freed to attack.

"We should fight our way through and jump," Rollan said. "It's our only chance."

Conor held up Anka with one shoulder and blocked an Oathbound with his free hand, sword meeting ax in a metallic clash. Briggan was a few steps ahead, fighting with a mountain lion. "Didn't you almost die in that same waterfall?"

Rollan jumped backward as an enemy blade sliced his arm. He would definitely need Jhi's help once they made it out of here—*if* they made it out. "There's a big difference between *almost* dying and actually dying," he said. He kicked the soldier in the shin, dropping him, then buried his dagger in the man. "I'd rather take my chance with the rapids."

"They'll just follow us!" Meilin shouted. She now wielded two swords, and was swinging them both to keep the attackers at bay.

Worthy gritted his fanged teeth, still focusing the sword's flames on Cordelia's group. He began to back up and butted against the statue, his back pressed against the black obsidian. Abeke watched as Worthy's face rose to meet the Euran hero's. As his chest swelled, she saw a change in his expression.

"Jump," he said. "I'll hold them off for as long as I can. Try to buy you some time."

Conor shook his head, his eyes wide. "Worthy—"

"Go!" he yelled. "You're wasting precious time."

Conor nodded, then he, Anka, and Briggan leaped through the waterfall. They screamed all the way down. The Oathbound nearest to them hesitated, then jumped after them.

Abeke tried not to dwell on wondering if her friends had made it. She yanked an arrow from a fallen Oathbound and rushed to Worthy's side.

"Rollan and Meilin, you go next," Abeke said. She fired another arrow into one of the Oathbound to their right. "I'll help Worthy hold them off."

Meilin hurled both her swords at the Oathbound she was holding at bay. The blades found their mark, slicing though the men's black uniforms. Then she back-flipped off the ledge into the water.

"Show-off," Rollan muttered, before leaping off after her.

Holding the sword with one hand, Worthy wiped his damp brow. The heat must have been brutal, but he hadn't let up yet. "So how many arrows do you have left?" he asked Abeke. "Maybe a hundred?"

She quickly counted the arrows lying at her feet. "More like three."

"I figured you'd say something like that." Looking up at the statue again, he said, "You and Uraza should make a break for it. I'm right behind you."

Abeke grabbed the last of the arrows and rushed to the edge of the cliff. When she turned around, she saw that Worthy had stopped using the sword's fire powers. Instead he faced the statue, the sword raised high above his head.

"What are you doing?" Abeke fired her last arrows at the Oathbound. They would reach the mouth of the cave in seconds.

"Remember what you said? United in our mission, but not necessarily in *how* we execute that mission?" He swung the sword over his head, gaining momentum. "Finish the mission. Find the other gifts."

"Worthy, wait!" she yelled. She knew what he was trying to do. "There's no way you can cut through that statue. It's made of solid stone."

"The wildcat had a ferocious roar, but she also had nails and teeth as sharp as diamonds." This time the entire sword glowed. The steel blade had turned shiny blue. "Tell Dawson I was a hero!"

Worthy brought the sword down on the statue. The blade sliced through the black stone with surprising ease, lopping off a chunk of Gransfen's leg. He swung again, completely severing one stone leg. The statue shifted and began to tilt. There was a loud rumble as boulders dropped from the ceiling.

"You fool!" Cordelia yelled, dodging falling debris. "What are you doing?"

"Being a hero!" Worthy shouted back as he sliced the statue one last time. The carving collapsed, as did the roof of the cave it was holding up. Worthy disappeared in an avalanche of boulders, debris, and dust.

Cracks splintered underneath Abeke's feet as the rest of the cave began to fall apart. Turning, she took a flying leap through the waterfall. She looked to her left to see Uraza jump as well, her body arching in the air.

They slammed into the water. Abeke felt like she'd been hit in the stomach with a hammer. Kicking as hard as she could, she reached for the sky while the rapids pulled her along. Surfacing, she caught sight of Uraza and quickly took in a breath before the swirling currents pulled her under again. Abeke crashed into a large submerged boulder, then ricocheted off another.

There was no navigating this river. She was at the mercy of the currents.

She surfaced again, and quickly took in another gulp of air. This time, she couldn't see the leopard. Was Uraza behind her? Ahead of her? Was she—?

Abeke's thoughts were interrupted by a feeling of weightlessness. She hung in the air, almost like she was floating, before her body crashed into the water below.

She had fallen over another waterfall.

Her vision became blurred and pain radiated throughout her limbs. She knew she was bleeding, but she didn't know how badly.

Her body was heavy, as was her mind. She felt herself sinking. Slipping. She tried kicking her legs, but they refused to work.

The water became darker. Her lungs screamed out in pain.

She almost gave up.

But then, something caught her eye. Below her. A flash of gold fur.

Uraza! And she was in trouble.

Ignoring the pain in her lungs, Abeke stretched out to the beast. A second later, the leopard disappeared onto Abeke's arm.

Abeke shook her head, trying to push away the blackness, and kicked toward the surface. She kicked harder than she'd ever kicked before. She pulled at the water, trying to grab it like handfuls of straw, using it to pull herself up toward the light. Toward air. Toward life.

She exploded past the surface. Opening her mouth, she swallowed gulp after gulp of air, her chest heaving with each breath.

She heard splashing around her, and opened her eyes. "We've got you," Conor said as he and Briggan swam to her. "You're safe."

The Great Wolf reached her first, his gray fur wet and slick. She wrapped her arms around him once he was near. "Thank you," she said, rubbing her face into the wolf's coat. Then she quickly looked up. "Where are the others?" she gasped at Conor. "Are they–?"

"They're on shore. Jhi is taking care of Meilin. She's got a bad gash on her leg." Swimming on the one side of Briggan while Conor held fast to the other, Abeke headed to shore. "What about Worthy?" Conor asked. "Is he right behind you?"

Abeke looked at her friend, then shook her head. "He's not coming."

Only a handful of Oathbound had made it out of the cave and over the waterfall. Conor and Meilin had been ready for a fight, but without their numbers or their leader behind them, the mercenaries had retreated into the trees.

Which was probably for the best. The battle had taken a wretched toll on their entire team. Everyone was covered in cuts and bruises, some worse than others. But their physical scars paled in comparison to the loss of Worthy.

Before they left, the Greencloaks chanced a trip back to the waterfall, hoping to find some way back into the cave, but it was completely sealed off. Abeke suggested using the Heart of the Land to dig through, but Meilin slowly shook her head.

"It's too powerful and imprecise. With a collapse like this, we'd probably end up causing even more cave-ins farther inside."

Finally, they collected their packs, bid farewell to their friend, and found a safe place to bed down for the night.

They started a fire. A roasted fish sat on the flames, but no one seemed particularly interested in eating. Or in talking. They just sat there, stewing in their own thoughts.

Finally, after hours of staring at the flames, Rollan

cleared his throat. "I've been thinking . . . you know, once the cave started collapsing, I bet there were a bunch of other cave openings that popped up," he said. "He's a small guy. He could have found a fissure to squeeze through."

Meilin reached out and took Rollan's hand. "Rollan, don't torture yourself. . . ."

"I know it sounds crazy, but hear me out," he continued. "All he had to do was get back to the big cavern, right? If he got there, then he had a chance to survive." Rollan looked around, waiting for someone to buy into his theory. "Right?" he asked, his voice softer.

"And the Wildcat's Claw is pretty powerful," Conor said. "He could probably cut his way out." Conor hugged Briggan as he spoke. "If that blade can cut through a solid stone statue, it can easily carve through a few fallen boulders."

Meilin sat up, being careful not to uncover the bandage on her leg. "Knowing Worthy, he's probably already out, hiding in the trees. Just waiting for the perfect opportunity to reveal himself."

"That's Worthy for you," Abeke added. "Always wanting to be the hero." Her voice caught as she spoke the words.

No one spoke again for a few minutes. The tears flowed freely down her friends' faces now, as well as her own. Abeke couldn't see Anka, but she was sure that she was crying, too.

"We have to find the next gift," Abeke said.

"What's the point?" Rollan asked. "We lost the sword. We were supposed to collect all the gifts, remember?"

Anka shook her head, the movement revealing the older Greencloak's position. "There's more to the gifts than we realized. They aren't just symbols; the bond tokens have real power. Olvan sent you after them for a reason. We've got no choice but to continue."

Meilin nodded. "We have to finish the mission. For Erdas. For Worthy."

"But where do we start?" Abeke asked. "Nilo and Zhong are huge regions. The gifts could be anywhere."

"Yes, I was thinking about that," Anka said. "We know the names of the other two items: Stormspeaker and the Dragon's Eye. So we need a library. Somewhere with a recorded history of the legends of Erdas," she said. "Any clues where that would be?"

"Greenhaven Castle comes to mind," Meilin said. "But since that's off-limits, the only other library I can think of is at the emperor's palace in Zhong. Which obviously is out of the question, too."

"I know of a place in Nilo that's filled with ancient books and records," Conor said. "As well as someone who's as old as the spirit animal bond itself."

Meilin groaned. "Don't say it," she warned. "Don't say it!"

As Conor smiled, Abeke realized that he looked a little like Worthy. "I think we need to see Takoda at the monastery," Conor continued. "He and the monks have an extensive library. Plus, there's someone ancient and clever we could also try talking to."

"And who is that?" Anka asked.

"Kovo," Meilin muttered, staring into the flames. "Kovo, the Great Betrayer."

Varian Johnson is the author of eight novels for children and young adults, including the middle-grade capers *The Great Greene Heist* and *To Catch a Cheat*. A former structural engineer, he now lives outside of Austin, Texas, with his family.

BOOK SEVEN

STORMSPEAKER

Now fugitives, the young heroes must clear their names
while evading the ruthless Oathbound. They head for
a hidden refuge of learning in Nilo, hoping to discover
the locations of the other two gifts. Guarding this
knowledge are their old friends Takoda and Xanthe,
along with Kovo the Ape.

With the Oathbound following close behind, can the
heroes risk branding their friends as traitors?

scholastic.com/spiritanimals